"Ah . . . aren't y

Alex's voice trailed off as Gretchen wandered across the kitchen. She was wearing only a soft white T-shirt that sensuously outlined her breasts and hips.

"No," Gretchen answered, looking at her bare feet. "I never wear slippers." She reached into the cupboard, and the T-shirt rode all the way up to the top of her thighs.

"Let me help you," Alex offered. But as she turned, their bodies touched, and instantly Alex's arms were around her in a tight embrace. His mouth met hers, his tongue teasingly caressing.

"Why did you do that?" she asked in a hoarse whisper when they broke apart. "You told me there wouldn't be any hanky-panky."

"What do you expect, running around half-nude?" he asked gruffly.

"There's absolutely nothing wrong with this T-shirt. As for the slippers . . ."

"Forget the slippers!" Alex exclaimed in frustration, drawing her close again.

Authors **Sally Siddon and Barbara Bradford**, a writing team already established in the Harlequin Superromance line, have now published their first Temptation. Sally, a former journalist, and Barbara, a former teacher, are both based in Virginia. *When Fortune Smiles* is sure to draw a lot of fans, as it is the ultimate in romance—the story of a young woman who finds love . . . *and* money!

When Fortune Smiles
SALLY BRADFORD

Harlequin Books

TORONTO • NEW YORK • LONDON
AMSTERDAM • PARIS • SYDNEY • HAMBURG
STOCKHOLM • ATHENS • TOKYO • MILAN

Published August 1989

ISBN 0-373-25363-X

1

GRETCHEN BAUER WAS SURE she'd never seen him before. So why was he standing there calmly inviting her into her own apartment?

He shot her a rakish grin. "Let me introduce myself," he said, extending his hand. "I'm Alex Carson, your new roommate."

Gretchen stared at the man's waiting hand, then looked up into his dark eyes. "You're who?"

"Your new roommate."

"You've got to be kidding," she whispered. But she had a gut feeling he wasn't. Her eyes searched his lightly tanned face with its symmetrical features and the shock of rumpled brown hair that fell across his broad forehead. "How did you get in here?"

"With your old roommate's key—actually my key, now," Alex explained. He stuffed both his hands into his back pockets, which made his jeans tighter.

Gretchen tried not to notice.

"Why don't you take off your coat?" he suggested. "If we're going to live together, we really should get acquainted."

"Let me get this straight." Gretchen looked him squarely in the eye. "You have somehow got the impression that you're going to live here? With me?"

"That's right."

Something about his tone—*smug* was a good word for it—sent Gretchen into orbit. She was flat broke and desperate for a roommate, but not desperate enough to consider a man, especially one who had just walked in off the street. "Alex—you did say your name was Alex?"

He nodded.

"Alex, there's been a big mistake." She drew herself up to her full five foot two inches, which put the dark curls of hair at the open neck of his shirt precisely at her eye level. "You absolutely cannot live here."

"I appreciate your reluctance," he replied, "but as you can see—" He gestured toward the living room. "I've already moved in."

"Oh, my God!" Gretchen gasped. She'd been so unnerved by him that she hadn't noticed anything else. Horrified, she looked around. Cardboard boxes were stacked floor to ceiling in front of the bay window. Her couch, her wonderful couch with the orange and yellow poppies, was littered with sports equipment—two tennis rackets, a bicycle helmet, skis and scuba gear. And in her moss-green chair, the one that matched the moss-green poppy leaves on the couch fabric, sat a gigantic aquarium along with an air filter, some plastic plants and a box of dried brine shrimp, presumably to feed the nonexistent fish. Overall, her cozy little apartment, on a quiet street in Arlington, Virginia, looked like a warehouse sale about to begin. "What is all that stuff?" she demanded.

"Just the things I'll be needing while I'm here," he answered nonchalantly.

If Gretchen had any doubts at all, that settled it. Anyone who could afford that array of expensive toys was not her type. "I can see that you've already moved in," she began with her jaw firmly set, "and now you can move right back out."

"Not that easy." His eyes, which were exactly the color of bittersweet chocolate, twinkled with amusement. "Why don't I take your coat and we'll sit down and talk about it? I can tell I'm not what you expected."

"You might say that."

He reached toward her, but Gretchen sidestepped him. "I can manage my own coat, thank you." She was having enough trouble without him coming any closer.

"Well, you're not what I'd expected, either," Alex observed bluntly. That was an understatement. He'd had no clue that Gretchen was such a knockout. She looked like something out of a fantasy. Her hair was blond, a very soft light blond, which made her fair skin appear all the more delicate. Her eyes, which seemed to have been colored the same blue as the summer sky, were set wide apart above a small upturned nose and slightly bowed red lips.

Alex felt a sense of anticipation building as he watched her unfasten the buttons of her long wool coat one by one. But nothing could have prepared him for the view when she slipped the coat off her shoulders and revealed a scanty, white sequined outfit that molded curves in all the right places. The outfit stopped just at the beginning of long, perfectly shaped legs, emphasized by the sheen of her stockings.

He swallowed hard and cleared his throat. "Do you always dress like that?"

"Like what?" Gretchen's eyes dropped to her bridal costume.

Alex's gaze followed hers. When she moved, the softness of her breasts was barely visible above the shimmering outfit. He took a deep breath. "I thought you were a first-grade teacher." He tried to focus on her face. "But you don't look like any first-grade teacher I ever saw."

Gretchen laughed. "I'd never go to school dressed like this, but I'm not teaching at the moment. I'm a performer—in a way."

"In what way?" Alex was beginning to wonder if he was getting mixed up with a stripper. Which, on second thought, could have its advantages. He started clearing off the couch. "Come on in and sit down."

Gretchen tossed her coat on top of the aquarium. Something had to be done. This man was acting as though he lived here, and even though she had to admit he was terribly attractive, sharing her apartment with him was out of the question. Despite her financial crisis—and it was a crisis—no way was she going to have a male roommate. "Now look, Mr. Carson," she began in a very firm voice.

He glanced up from shoving the rubber strap into his swim mask and shot her that grin. "If you're going to be formal, it's Dr. Carson," he said disarmingly.

"All right, *Dr.* Carson—you're a doctor?"

"No, actually—" He moved his bike helmet and tennis rackets from the couch to the floor, then looked at Gretchen. "Actually, I'm a dentist."

"You're a *dentist*?" Gretchen could have handled a doctor, but a *dentist*? She shuddered.

Alex looked offended. "You have something against dentists?"

"No, of course not," Gretchen answered quickly. "At least nothing personal. I've never talked to a dentist except one with a drill in his hand."

"That makes us even. I've never talked to a first-grade teacher who wears so few clothes."

Gretchen had rather liked her bridal ensemble until that moment. Suddenly self-conscious, she sat on the end of the couch as far from Alex as possible. "This is just a costume. I already told you that." She didn't know why she was explaining to him, but for some reason she felt compelled to continue. "I'm between teaching jobs at the mo-

ment—actually I was destaffed in the cutbacks last fall—
and so I'm working for Shenanigans."

"What's that?" Alex asked curiously. It sounded like a
bar. Maybe she really was a stripper. His eyes followed her
plunging neckline, which revealed . . . objectively it didn't
reveal much of anything, but it sure did a lot for the imagination.

"Shenanigans is a spinoff of the old singing telegrams,"
Gretchen told him. "We perform at parties, deliver greet-
ings and balloons for birthdays, anniversaries, hospital
patients—that sort of thing."

"You go to hospitals dressed like that?"

Gretchen laughed, and the melodic sound filled the
room. "Not quite. When I go to hospitals I'm Clara the
Clown," she explained. "Tonight I had a bachelor party,
so I wore the wedding outfit. The costume fits the job."

Alex shook his head. She had the strangest job he'd ever
heard of. "You mean if I want balloons delivered to my
partner on his birthday, or if I'm looking for a stripper, all
I have to do is call Shenanigans and they'll take care of it?"

"Balloons, yes, strippers, no. We don't—" Gretchen
stopped in midsentence, her blue eyes flashing. "You
thought I was a stripper!"

"Sorry," he mumbled. As she drew herself up straight,
the top of her costume inched downward, revealing the
cleavage between her softly rounded breasts. Alex looked
away. He didn't understand why that scanty outfit had
such a dramatic effect on his imagination.

Gretchen wasn't going to let him off that easily. "I can
guess what you're thinking, and you're wrong. Dead
wrong. The most exciting thing I do is pop out of wedding cakes."

Alex felt himself begin to chuckle. The explanation
hadn't helped at all. He'd moved in thinking he was going

to camp out in some first-grade teacher's spare room and instead he was hooked up with a flaky broad who jumped out of cakes. The more he thought about the irony of it, the funnier it got.

"Go ahead. Laugh. I don't care," Gretchen said defensively. "You may think it's funny, but it helps pay the bills."

"I suppose it would," he answered, still chuckling.

"You obviously don't understand something like that," she retorted. "You probably make a mint every time you stick your drill into someone's mouth, which is no doubt why you can afford to own all this junk you've dumped in my living room."

"I've worked damn hard for what I have," Alex shot back. He realized he was on the defensive and he didn't like it. "If you gathered up everything you have in this apartment," he said with a sweep of his arm, "your stuff would look like a hell of a lot, too."

"My point exactly." Gretchen sprang to her feet. "This apartment isn't big enough for both of us."

"You've convinced me." To bad, he thought, with a glance toward Gretchen. She had such intriguing possibilities. He stood abruptly and started down the hall toward the spare bedroom. "I'll start looking for another place tomorrow."

"And by the time I get home tomorrow night, you'd better have found it," Gretchen yelled after him. She stalked into her own bedroom and slammed the door. The gall of him, she thought as she took off her costume. Moving into her apartment and acting as if he owned the place, as if she'd take in anyone off the street. She needed a roommate, all right, and fast, before the rent was due. But not a man. When she lived with a man, it was going to be a man she was in love with, not some dentist.

THE FOLLOWING NIGHT, Gretchen's high heels clicked rhythmically as she walked through the courtyard that separated the two red brick apartment buildings. It was nearly midnight, and she was exhausted. She'd spent a free hour between jobs juggling her finances, and every way she figured it, she came up short. Even working long hours, the money wasn't enough. Too bad about Alex Carson, she thought for the hundredth time. If she had someone to split the rent with, she could barely scrape by. But she'd figure out something, she told herself. She always did.

She unlocked the door to her apartment and opened it slowly. Everything was dark. The only sound was the familiar hiss of the steam heat from the radiator in the corner of the living room.

So he had moved out. "Good riddance," she muttered to herself, wondering why she didn't feel the sweet sense of victory she'd expected. Maybe she was just tired. She stepped inside and shoved the door shut with her foot. What she needed was a good night's sleep. Without bothering to turn on the light, Gretchen headed directly for the bedroom.

The crash would have wakened the dead. And, if it didn't, her scream would have. Alex was out of bed like a shot. "Gretchen! Gretchen, where are you?" He fumbled for the light switch and, when he found it, quickly assessed the damage.

Gretchen was still standing. His bike wasn't. Neither appeared hurt, but she sure looked mad. "Are you all right?" he asked hesitantly.

She glared first at him, then at the sleek black and silver racing bike, which lay on the yellow shag carpet with its back wheel still spinning in the air. "What is that?" she demanded, pointing at the bike. She leaned over to rub her bruised shin. "It practically killed me."

"I guess I should have warned you," Alex apologized. "I rode it from the office today."

"But what is it doing in my apartment?"

He shrugged. "No other place to keep it. Expensive bikes get stolen if you leave them outside overnight."

All the other junk and now a bicycle. What kind of a pushover did he think she was? She was about to level him when she took a good look at him for the first time since she'd come home. She promptly wished she hadn't. He apparently slept in sweatpants and nothing else. She assumed he'd been asleep when she came in. His shoulders were just as broad and just as solid as they'd looked with his clothes on. The dark hair that had curled out at the neck of his shirt also covered his chest in a V shape, she discovered, narrowing as it approached his navel and then disappearing inside the sweats, which rode low on his hips.

Gretchen leaned over to pick up her net bridal veil, which had fallen out of her pocket when she collided with the bike. Staring at Alex Carson's body was not going to solve a thing. She had already decided she wouldn't share the apartment with him under any circumstances. Even if he weren't a man, there wasn't room for him, not with all the stuff he owned. Gretchen pulled at the veil, but it was caught on the bike gears. She tugged harder and heard it start to rip.

"Damn!" she muttered.

"Do you need some help?"

"That would be nice," she said coolly, "especially considering it's your bike that is ripping my veil."

"I am sorry about that," Alex said as he knelt down and began deftly unhooking the netting.

"You're not supposed to be here, either," she reminded him. "You promised to move out today."

He extracted the wisp of net he'd been working on and moved to another before he answered. "If I remember correctly, you were the one who said I was moving out today. I was the one who said I'd start looking for another place."

"And?"

"And I didn't find one," he said. Whistling softly, he continued slowly working the netting free of the gears.

His fingers were supple, Gretchen noticed, like those of a surgeon or a pianist. Or a dentist. She studied his angular face, his brow furrowed as he leaned over his work. Then she noticed his forearms, which were surprisingly muscular. He smelled of soap and a hint of musk cologne, altogether a very male smell.

"You know, you could have at least phoned instead of just moving in," Gretchen pointed out. "That would have saved you dragging all this stuff in here and then having to haul it right back out."

"You think I didn't try to phone?" he countered. "I called every night and you didn't answer. So I figured I'd do you a favor and go ahead and move in."

"Do me a favor?" He just didn't give up. "You move into my apartment when I'm not home, dump your stuff all over my living room, booby-trap my front door with your bicycle and you call that doing me a favor?"

"I really am sorry about the bike," Alex said sincerely. As the last bit of netting slipped free, Alex straightened up.

Gretchen hadn't realized she was standing quite so close to him. As he handed her the veil, their eyes met and held and, in that instant, she was acutely aware of him and everything about him. A shiver ran through her. Turning away, she thanked him, but her voice sounded strange to her.

Gretchen could feel Alex watching her as she stuffed the veil into her coat pocket then dropped the coat over an old rocking chair, the only piece of furniture in the room with nothing piled on it. As ridiculous as it sounded, he seemed to be all around her, his presence filling the entire apartment until he was so close it was hard to catch her breath. She was obviously not dealing with the situation at all effectively. The longer he was in the apartment with her, the less effective she seemed to be.

She walked to the far corner of the living room, threading her way around the boxes, and stood with her back against the radiator. That was the reason she'd come, she told herself, to be close to the warmth of the radiator, not just to get away from him. Across the wasteland of boxes, she faced him, determined to stand firm in her decision.

"Dr. Carson—"

"Cut it out, Gretchen," he interrupted impatiently.

"All right . . . Alex. But whatever I'm going to call you, we need to come to an understanding. You have to move out. Now. Tomorrow. You simply cannot live here."

"I think we need to discuss that," he replied. He'd given the situation some thought, too. Actually, that was the only thing he'd had on his mind all day. And the more he thought about it, the more he liked the idea of living in Gretchen Bauer's spare bedroom. Or at least starting out there.

"What's to discuss? You simply can't live here," Gretchen repeated. She wished she weren't wearing the bridal outfit again. From the way he kept looking at it, she knew it was getting the way of a serious conversation.

"There's something I forgot to tell you." Alex sat down at one end of the couch, which was still cleared off from the night before. "It could have an effect on your decision."

"I've made my decision," Gretchen said firmly, "and nothing, but nothing will change my mind."

"Even if I tell you I've already paid the March rent?"

"You what?"

"I paid the March rent." He could see he'd caught her by surprise, which was exactly what he'd intended to do. "I paid the March rent," he repeated, smiling because he knew he'd hit a vulnerable point. "I'd been told you were a little short of cash so I picked up the entire first month myself." He settled back comfortably. "I figured I should do something to help make up for the inconvenience."

Damn! Gretchen thought. Now what was she going to do? She couldn't pay him back, at least not right away. Of course, he had no way of knowing what desperate financial straits she was in. She hesitated, unsure how to proceed. She'd always prided herself on her ability to get out of tight spots, and she'd certainly had lots of practice. But dealing with Alex Carson was going to test even her expertise. Gretchen met his dark brown eyes and realized she was going to have to be blunt. "This is nothing personal, Alex," she began in a confidential tone. She walked slowly across the room and sat on the opposite end of the couch from Alex. "I want you to understand that."

He nodded.

"The problem is something you can't help." She paused to emphasize the point she was about to make. "The problem is you're a man."

"So?" Alex shrugged. "I've never considered that a problem."

"Well, I do," Gretchen declared. "I'm not ready to live with a man, especially one I've barely met. You'll have to try someone else."

His eyebrows shot up. "Wait a minute, exactly what do you mean by that?"

"Just what it sounds like. I'm not into bed hopping. It's not my thing." She wished she'd stayed over by the radiator to discuss it. She had a much harder time concentrating when she was sitting there on the couch with Alex sprawled out at the other end, minus his shirt.

"If you think I'm here to drag you off to bed—" He stopped, not because the prospect was so shocking, but because he rather liked it. In truth, that hadn't been his intention and still wasn't. But every time she got close to him, even down at the other end of the couch, it did cross his mind.

"Then why are you so determined to live here?" Gretchen asked him. "There must be a dozen other places that would be more your style, judging from all your stuff." She glanced around the room.

"Nope, this is perfect," Alex said. "All I want is some place where I don't have a lease. Some place temporary to stay till my condominium is finished."

"How temporary?"

"Just a few months." He sat forward and said in a persuasive tone, "I'll bet we could work this out if we tried, Gretchen."

"Alex, I've already told you—"

"Why don't we do a trial run for a couple of weeks? Then if you want me to look for another place, I will. Of course," he added, "I might not be able to find anything right away because I'm tied up at the office all day."

Gretchen was tempted. Not having to deal with the March rent would take a big load off her budget. Besides, he was only going to be there a few months. And she did have to admit that Alex wasn't personally objectionable. As long as he stayed in his own bedroom.... She met his eyes and looked quickly away. That could become a problem. Then she thought about what he'd said. "You're at the office all day, every day?" she repeated.

"Pretty much, except weekends."

"That means you'd be gone all day."

"So?"

"I'm here in the daytime. Most of my jobs are late afternoon and evening." Gretchen stared at him with an expression of sudden inspiration. "That means we wouldn't see each other—"

"Practically at all," Alex finished for her. "I get up early on Saturdays—how about you?"

"I sleep till noon," she informed him. "And I deliver balloons to the hospital on Saturday afternoon."

"I'm gone most of Sunday—handball, tennis, scuba diving lessons," he said.

"I like to stay home on Sunday to throw in laundry, do my nails, that sort of thing," Gretchen added, looking at him thoughtfully. This living arrangement was beginning to sound almost feasible. With their schedules they'd barely notice each other.

"You think we can work something out?" Alex asked. He really didn't want to put anything more in storage and he was less than enthusiastic about living in a furnished room, even temporarily. Besides, her apartment had everything he wanted for the short term—including Gretchen.

"I suppose we could try it," she agreed cautiously. "But only if you clear all this stuff out of the living room."

"Where would you suggest I put it?" he inquired.

As far as Gretchen was concerned, what he did with it was his problem. "Put it in your bedroom, in storage—I don't care what you do with it, but you can't leave it here."

"I've already put almost everything I own in storage," Alex explained.

Gretchen gasped. "You mean you own even more?"

"Of course, I own more." He couldn't figure out why she had such a hang-up about his personal possessions. "How do you suppose I'm going to furnish my condominium?"

"I can't imagine." Furnishing a condominium wasn't one of Gretchen's problems, and she didn't expect it to be any time soon.

"If we're going to share this apartment, I get half the space," Alex declared.

Gretchen frowned. The request was reasonable, but she didn't like it. "There are some empty drawers in the chest over there, and half of the storage closet is empty, too," she said grudgingly. "But the bicycle won't fit. It has to go."

"No way," he said firmly. "That's my transportation. The bicycle stays."

"You don't have a car?" With all his other possessions, he must have a car.

"Sure I do, but I ride the bike to work. Aerobic exercise."

"Your office is near here?"

"About ten miles. That's one reason I liked this location. It's just about the right distance for my bike."

Gretchen wasn't sure she'd heard him right. In fact she was virtually positive she hadn't. "You ride a bicycle ten miles to the office and ten miles home every day?" No wonder his body was so trim and taut and his thigh muscles were apparent even under his sweats.

"Why not? What do you do for exercise besides pop out of cakes?"

"I get plenty of exercise," Gretchen replied quickly. She was suddenly aware that the only place she didn't take her car was to the convenience store, and that was across the street. "And I manage without a bicycle in the middle of the living room."

Alex grinned. "I'm sure you do," he told her. He stood up and stretched. The sweatpants inched lower. "Now, if you don't mind, I'm going back to bed where any normal person should be at this hour." He started down the hall, then turned to Gretchen. "By the way," he added, "we're out of hand soap. Where do you keep it?"

"In the bathroom cabinet," she answered automatically. "Wait a minute! We've only got one bathroom."

"So I noticed. I hung your panty hose over the shower rod—the ones you left soaking in the sink."

Gretchen felt her face flush. "You were the one who said this living arrangement wouldn't be any problem," she reminded him.

"Right," he agreed, disappearing into the bathroom and closing the door firmly behind him.

Gretchen gathered up her coat, shoes and veil and started toward her bedroom, glaring at the closed bathroom door as she passed it. From now on she'd make sure she got to the bathroom first.

2

GRETCHEN SAT in the moss-green chair and glowered at a large striped angelfish peering out from behind a floating sprig of seaweed. She didn't want an aquarium full of fish in her living room any more than she wanted a yuppie dentist in her spare bedroom, and they had both been there for three days now.

But the fish weren't the real problem and, at the moment, neither was Alex. Gretchen stared glumly at the papers stacked in her lap—a credit-card bill, two rejected loan applications, her bank statement, showing a balance of $17.62, and a letter from her sister. The real problem was money.

She read Joyce's letter one more time even though she knew it by heart. "Dear Gretch," it began. Joyce was the only one who had ever called her Gretch. She read on:

Exams were a bear but I made it. A few more months and they'll call me Dr. Joyce. I hate to push you for the rest of the money—you've done so much already—but unless I pay my tuition soon they're threatening not to let me graduate. Some day I'll find a way to repay you.

Love you,
Joyce

Gretchen slowly folded the letter and put it back in the envelope. There wasn't anyone else who could help. She and Joyce had made their plans years ago after their father had walked out, leaving their mother to support the family. Gretchen, who was three years older, would go to college first. Then she would begin teaching, and her salary would help get Joyce through medical school and on the way to being a pediatric cardiologist. Gretchen had thought they'd make it until she lost her teaching job. Now she was trying to get along on the Shenanigans money, which had been supposed to be extra. It wasn't enough.

The pump at the back of Alex's aquarium hummed steadily, sending a steady column of bubbles rising through the clear water. Gretchen watched two small fish dart by, sleek blue specimens she had never seen before. No doubt they cost a fortune, she decided, like everything else Alex had. He could probably just write a check and Joyce's problems would be solved.

Gretchen considered that possibility for a few moments and rejected it. She barely knew Alex Carson. Then she thought about it again. One of the reasons she'd let Alex move in was that he had money and she didn't. He might at least have some suggestions for her, and she could use any advice she could get. She heard a thumping on the stairs and then a key turned in the front door. She looked up expectantly.

"You're home early," she greeted Alex, making no comment as he rolled his bike across the yellow shag carpet and parked it in front of the closet. That bike probably cost almost as much as her secondhand Volkswagen.

"Yeah, I play tennis on Wednesday afternoon when the office is closed. I forgot to tell you."

"That's nice," Gretchen answered, smiling at him.

Alex hung his helmet over his bike seat. Could this be the same woman who ridiculed his sports equipment, hated his bike and refused to let him live in her apartment unless he practically swore he'd never be there when she was? Something had changed. "You seem in high spirits this afternoon," he observed.

Gretchen's smile faded. "No, not really," she responded. "Actually I'm very worried."

She'd just thrown a cue line if he'd ever heard one. He was supposed to say, "What are you worried about?" She would tell him, and then he was supposed to come up with a solution. Nice and tidy. "What seems to be the problem?" he asked warily.

"Money," Gretchen answered in a barely audible whisper. This was harder than she'd expected. Why was it people could discuss sex and religion and politics and yet it was so hard to talk about money?

"Money," he repeated, laughing. "Yeah, you and everyone else. No one ever has enough money." He started down the hall toward the bedroom.

Gretchen was sorry she'd ever considered confiding in him. Even if he had money he was a self-centered, uncaring boor. She'd solve her own problems without any help from him. "And another thing," she called after him. "Can't you put this stupid aquarium in your bedroom instead of in the living room?"

Alex chuckled. He'd wondered how long it was going to take her to react to the aquarium. "The fish wouldn't do well in the bedroom. Too much sunlight. Sunlight promotes the growth of algae."

"Then close the curtain."

"Half this place is mine, remember? And the only thing I've put in the living room is the fish."

"You could have at least asked." He also could have at least discussed her problem. If he wouldn't help that was one thing, but he could have at least listened.

"I've got to get ready or I'm going to be late for my tennis date," Alex said. "Keep watching the fish. Maybe you'll learn to like them."

Gretchen watched him disappear into his bedroom. She was never going to like fish. Especially these fish. She was going to get rid of them and Alex Carson along with them just as soon as she could.

When Alex came out of the bedroom, he was wearing a burgundy warm-up suit with a designer logo on the pocket and carrying a tennis racket under his arm. He could have been a tennis pro, even to the light tan on his face, no doubt from all the time he spent outside. His hair, which was usually so unruly, was slicked back. Gretchen wondered whether this tennis date was female, not that it mattered. She wasn't interested.

"See you later—that is, if you're going to be home tonight," Alex said.

Gretchen didn't answer.

Still watching her, Alex opened the apartment door and nearly collided with a tall redheaded woman wearing a nurse's uniform and carrying a large mug of coffee.

"Whoops! Sorry," he apologized. "You were coming to see Gretchen?"

"I'm Trudy Munson. I live next door." Trudy backed away, never taking her eyes off Alex. "But I wouldn't want to interrupt anything."

"No problem," Alex assured her. "I was just leaving." He stepped aside to let Trudy enter, then wheeled his bike out and closed the door.

"Wow!" Trudy exclaimed as soon as he was gone. "Who was that hunk?"

"His name is Alex Carson."

Still clutching her coffee mug, Trudy plopped down on the couch across from Gretchen. "I've lived next door to you for two years, I pass by on a regular basis on my way to and from the hospital, and I never saw anything like that go out of here. And in the middle of the afternoon!"

"It's nothing like that, believe me," Gretchen assured her. "He's just living here temporarily."

Trudy ran her free hand through her short red curls. "I see. Just living here. Just like that."

Gretchen shook her head. "No, not just like that. He's a dentist," she explained. From the expression on Trudy's face, she realized that didn't help at all. "What I mean is, he's a stubborn, yuppie dentist who is paying half the rent. Are you with me so far?"

Trudy nodded, but still looked blank. "Where did you pick up a dentist?"

"I didn't pick him up," Gretchen retorted. "When I got home from work the other night, he'd already moved in. I'd never even met him before that."

Trudy rolled her eyes skyward. "Why can't anything like that ever happen to me? Those shoulders...and those big brown bedroom eyes? God, what I'd do for those eyes!"

"As far as I'm concerned, you can have them, and him, too," Gretchen said. "Except for one thing."

"No doubt the very thing I have in mind."

Gretchen ignored her. "The only reason I let him stay is that he has already paid the March rent, and you know how broke I am."

"You mean he's got money?"

"You should see all the rest of his junk," Gretchen said, curling her legs under her. "This aquarium is only the beginning. He can't be starving."

Trudy lit a cigarette and leaned forward, her voice rising in her excitement. "Then maybe he's your answer. The money you need for Joyce—have you considered trying to get it from him?"

Gretchen nodded. "I considered it," she mumbled. She was almost ashamed to admit that, even to Trudy. She had never, even at the lowest points in her life, asked anyone for money.

"And?" Trudy prompted.

"And I tried to bring up the subject, just to ask his advice, and he brushed me off. Didn't even want to discuss it."

"Too bad," Trudy said. "He looks like your best bet next to winning the lottery. The pot is up to two million dollars this week, you know."

"Damn, I'd like to have two million dollars." Gretchen sighed. "Just think, Trudy. It would solve everything." Gretchen loved the lottery dream. Every Saturday, when she bought her lottery ticket, which she did faithfully each week no matter how tight money was, she let herself pretend for a few minutes that it had actually happened. Her number was the one that came up for the jackpot. She was showered with congratulations, and as her hand was reached out to accept that check, she knew her worries were over. She'd have all the money Joyce could ever need, everything would be taken care of, and she wouldn't have to think about how to pay the bills for the rest of her life.

Gretchen stared at the silver angelfish, which she disliked even more than before. Alex Carson had probably never wondered how to pay his bills. Life really wasn't fair. "I don't know what I'm going to do about Joyce," she mused, half to Trudy and half to herself. "I got another letter from her. She has to have the tuition money, and I guess I gave her the impression I already have things worked out. I haven't told her I lost my job."

"Listen, I've got two hundred dollars socked away toward a vacation," Trudy offered. "You're welcome to it."

"Thanks, Trudy." Gretchen smiled at her friend. "But I need more like five thousand dollars."

"That *is* a problem! You're sure there's no way Joyce can dig up something herself?"

"She's used up all her grants and she's in hock from last year. It's up to me."

"Then maybe you should try to borrow the money," Trudy suggested.

Gretchen picked up the rejected loan applications. "Every bank in northern Virginia has turned me down flat. I don't have enough collateral to borrow a quarter for a cup of coffee."

"No," Trudy said, finishing her coffee, "I don't mean from the bank. There's this hole-in-the-wall finance place that just opened up on Filmore Avenue. I go by it on my way to the hospital."

Gretchen looked up. "Really?"

"It looks like a pretty sleazy operation, but they've got big signs advertising easy loans. No collateral needed."

Gretchen didn't care how sleazy it looked. Money was money. "Just give me the directions, and if nothing turns up by the end of the week, I'll try it."

"It really is a crummy place," Trudy added hesitantly.

"I'm desperate, Trudy," Gretchen told her. "I'll do anything to keep Joyce in school." Anything, she added silently, except talk to Alex Carson about it. She was never going to try to discuss anything important with him again.

FOR THE REST OF THE WEEK Gretchen managed to avoid Alex. By the time she woke up in the morning, Alex, his bicycle and his accompanying helmet with the funny little side mirrors were long gone. The only time she had to worry about tripping over his ten-speed was when she came in late at night. She'd already learned to come through the apartment door slowly and cautiously.

Although Alex was never around, his presence was everywhere. Her once tidy medicine cabinet was cluttered with an assortment of male toiletries. His after-shave lotion, shaving cream and razor filled the bottom shelf, and containers of aspirin, vitamins and a bottle of rubbing alcohol took most of the second shelf. The top of the vanity was cluttered with a bottle of hydrogen peroxide, a Water Pik, dental floss, baking soda and salt, which meant her skin lotion and dusting powder were relegated to a small space near the back.

The baking soda and salt especially irritated Gretchen, so she slapped an adhesive-backed note on the mirror:

Alex—
Please take the food back to the kitchen

There was an answering note on the mirror the next morning:

Gretchen—
Apparently you aren't aware that baking soda and salt are an important part of a good oral hygiene program and, therefore, do belong in the bathroom.

Taped next to the note was a cute little pamphlet outlining a plan to prevent gum disease.

"Gum disease," Gretchen muttered as she tore the pamphlet into tiny pieces and flushed them down the toilet. "If he wants to lose sleep over gum disease, that's his problem." She deliberately did a cursory job of brushing her teeth, but allowed herself one quick look in the mirror to make sure her gums weren't bleeding.

The bathroom wasn't the only problem. Her open, sunny kitchen was cluttered with a variety of expensive yuppie appliances—a food processor, an electric wok, a combination coffee bean grinder and coffee maker and a computerized microwave. Initially she was simply annoyed because they took up space. But on Saturday morning she discovered how much she really disliked them.

She was in the midst of a lovely dream about a money tree when a roaring sound jarred her awake. It took only a moment for her to determine that the sound was coming from Alex's food processor. "Shut that stupid thing off," she groaned.

Alex obviously didn't hear her. "Shut it off," she said again, shouting this time. Sleepily she closed her eyes. She was definitely not ready to get up. She'd done three shows the previous night, all of them big bachelor parties in different sections of the city. Her feet still ached from those spiky high heels she wore with the bridal costume.

The food processor roared again. "Damn," Gretchen muttered. Since she obviously wasn't going back to sleep, the only choice left was to get out of bed. With a yawn, she stood up, stretched and pulled down the oversize T-shirt she wore instead of pajamas. If she couldn't sleep, she might as well eat something and get ready to go to the hospital for her Saturday afternoon clown show. Barefooted, she headed toward the kitchen for a large cup of coffee.

Alex looked up from the food processor when he heard Gretchen's footsteps. "There's fresh coffee in the pot at..." His voice trailed off as he took a good look at his roommate. She was wearing nothing, at least nothing he could see, but a white cotton T-shirt that stopped well above her knees. Alex cleared his throat and finished his sentence. "Coffee, at the end of the counter."

Gretchen wandered sleepily across the kitchen and filled her mug from the steaming pot. "Thanks," she said, yawning again. She leaned against the refrigerator and took a long sip of her coffee.

Alex couldn't stop watching her. Seeing her in the showy bride costume had been one thing, but seeing her in this outfit was something else. The soft cotton fell sensuously over her curves, outlining every contour of her breasts and hips, ending just a few inches down on her shapely legs and leaving very little to the imagination. Did she have any idea how she looked or what effect she might have on a man?

Alex cleared his throat again. "Ah..." He paused. "Aren't you cold?"

Gretchen looked down at her bare feet and wiggled her toes on the linoleum floor. "No," she answered. "I never wear slippers." What business of his was it anyway? She glanced up as he turned away and really saw him for the first time. He didn't look much like someone who spent his life worrying about gum disease. His shoulders were a little too broad and his arms too powerful under his red and blue rugby shirt. His body fit too well into his jeans. Something was definitely wrong when a man looked sexy with a food processor, but this one did.

Alex had lost track of his yogurt shake almost entirely, and not because Gretchen wasn't wearing slippers. Her bare feet were the least of his concerns. When she'd first walked into the kitchen, he'd been so overcome by the T-shirt that he hadn't seen anything else. Now he noticed that her huge blue eyes sparkled, and her cheeks were blushed pink. Her lips, bare of makeup, were ripe and luscious.

He pulled the plastic top off a pint of strawberries. Gretchen was still drinking her coffee. Her hair, blond and tousled around her face, looked as if she'd just climbed out of bed. More accurately, she looked exactly as if she'd just come from a delicious romp between the sheets. Alex felt a tightening in his groin. Damn, she was beautiful. He hadn't bargained for this. He tried hard to focus on the strawberries he was dropping into the food processor.

Gretchen looked hungrily at the strawberries for a moment before she walked up behind Alex and peered over his shoulder. "What are you making?" she asked curiously.

Alex could feel the warmth of her body next to his. "A strawberry-yogurt shake," he answered. The knife slipped and he nearly cut his thumb.

"What a waste of strawberries!" Gretchen shuddered, and her breasts jiggled against his back. "How can you possibly eat yogurt?" She moved away from him and reached for the box of flavored cereals on the top shelf of the cupboard.

Alex tensed. That was worse. Now her body was stretched out, and her breasts were high and firm. The T-shirt had pulled all the way up to the top of her thighs and barely covered her cute little.... Suddenly Alex wondered if she was wearing anything at all underneath that damned T-shirt, specifically panties. He didn't have a chance to find out. She set a bowl on the counter and filled it with a vile mixture of pink, yellow and orange flakes of cereal. Then she reached across him for the carton of milk, and her breast brushed his arm.

"Excuse me," she said.

Alex swallowed hard. All he wanted to do was take hold of her and wrap himself around her sexy body. Instead he stood close to the counter and poured his shake into a tall glass. When she took her bowl of cereal to the table and picked up the newspaper, he quickly sat down opposite her, relieved that the lower half of his body was hidden by the table.

"That's a lousy breakfast," he muttered.

"I suppose nutrition is another one of your crusades, along with gum disease?" Gretchen retorted, leafing through the newspaper.

"Gingivitis is a primary cause of early tooth loss," he answered irritably. "And so is a diet loaded with sugar."

"My teeth are just fine, thank you," Gretchen answered. She was still sorting through sections of the paper that were spread haphazardly across the table. "In fact my teeth are in a whole lot better shape than my bathroom, which used to be very neat until you spread your stuff all over it."

"Our bathroom," he corrected her. "I live here, too."

"Temporarily."

"You'll get no argument from me."

"Good. Don't get any ideas this living arrangement is going to last," she warned him. "Have you seen Section C of the paper?"

Alex glanced toward the wastebasket. "That could be the section I used to clean out my wok this morning. There wasn't anything important in it."

"What do you mean there wasn't anything important in it? That's the section with the winning lottery numbers!"

"You play the lottery?"

Not answering, Gretchen dug through the wastebasket. Alex drank his shake and concentrated on not looking at her.

"If I weren't short of cash, you wouldn't be living here at all, and I wouldn't have to dig my newspaper out of the garbage," she complained.

Alex wasn't about to ask why she was so strapped for money. She'd tried to bring it up once before, and he'd avoided the issue. Not that he wasn't sympathetic. But he'd learned a long time ago that the quickest way to end a friendship was to talk about money when you had it and the other person didn't.

"You're sure you put the whole section of the paper in here?" she demanded, digging deeper into the overflowing wastebasket.

"Here, let me help you," he offered, standing up. He supposed it was reasonable that she might be irritated because part of the newspaper was missing. But as soon as he bent down beside her, he knew he'd made a mistake. Her body was warm and sensual, and her hair held the scent of that cologne she wore. He stood up, but at the same moment so did she. Their bodies were touching, and then his arms were around her and she was tight against him.

Gretchen's response was instantaneous. The words on the tip of her tongue died without ever being spoken. She couldn't even remember what they were. A very specific heat, swirling downward, made it clear why his presence had been so unsettling to her all morning. She felt her cheeks flush, and as she looked upward his mouth met hers and she stopped thinking altogether.

Alex's chest was hard against her breasts. She felt the fresh-shaven skin on his face and smelled his after-shave, the same smell that sometimes lingered in the bathroom in the morning. His tongue teasingly caressed her lips, and she let her whole body press against him until the heat inside her became still more pervasive. His mouth was wet and welcoming; his eyes were closed. Then suddenly her mind slipped back in gear and her body stiffened. She felt Alex shaking as his mouth left hers and she separated her body from him.

Abruptly he stepped backward and let her go. He found himself looking down into her very large blue eyes, wide open beneath long lashes, and reflecting the same desire that coursed through him. He knew she was about to deny how she felt, but he also knew those eyes weren't lying.

"Why did you do that?" Her voice was a hoarse whisper.

"What do you expect, running around dressed like that?" he answered gruffly. He snatched the newspaper from the floor where he had dropped it and held it in front of him.

"You told me all you wanted was a place to stay, that there wouldn't be any of this," she said accusingly. She wished she could stop her heart from pounding. He'd had no right to kiss her and make her feel like that.

"If you'd been wearing clothes, this wouldn't have happened."

"I am wearing clothes," Gretchen answered angrily. "There's absolutely nothing wrong with this T-shirt. And as for the slippers . . ."

"Screw the slippers!" Alex exclaimed and stalked out of the kitchen.

Moments later, Gretchen heard the front door slam, followed by the thumping of Alex's bike wheel on the hall stairs. Maybe he wouldn't come back at all. The thought twisted oddly inside her as she walked to her bedroom.

ALEX WAS ON HIS BIKE and moving as soon as he hit the front sidewalk. He rode steadily, his thoughts hopscotching but always returning to Gretchen and the strange scene in the kitchen. He had never, in all his thirty years, lost control of himself. Actually he hadn't lost control this time, either, but he'd been on the edge. He'd wanted her. If she'd been wearing something other than that damned T-shirt....

But Gretchen wasn't the first woman he'd seen scantily clothed. Or naked for that matter. None of the others had made him behave like a horny adolescent. Alex thought about the T-shirt teasing the top of Gretchen's thighs and wondered again if she'd had panties underneath. He pedaled harder. Those images were likely to be dangerous for a man on a bike.

Although it was technically still winter, the weather was mild, and Alex rode for nearly two hours along the bike path that paralleled the Potomac River. Finally he grabbed a sandwich at a Greek deli and headed toward his office. For the past several months, he and his partner had alternated Saturday mornings running a free dental clinic for needy neighborhood kids. On this particular Saturday, he'd agreed to come in for a few minutes in the afternoon to see a little girl who couldn't get there in the morning. He wouldn't have done it for just anyone, but Susan was one of his favorites. Now he was glad he had the appointment for another reason: maybe it would take his mind off Gretchen.

Alex caught sight of the little girl when he was still a block away, her pigtails streaming behind her as she raced down the street toward the lamppost in front of his office.

"Look at my new roller skates, Dr. Carson," she called to him as he got off his bike. "And look at me. I can fly."

He caught her as she sailed into him and swung her off her feet. "You're really good," he said admiringly as he set her down. "But, tell me something. Have you learned how to stop yet?"

"No, but I will," she promised. "That's what Grandpa asked me, too."

Susan skated along beside Alex toward a white-haired man with a cane who stood near the door to the office. "Thanks for coming in, Doc," the old man said, smiling proudly at his granddaughter.

"Glad to do it, Mr. Halvorsen," Alex assured him. "First time this week I've had a chance to work on a patient in roller skates."

"We got them at the thrift shop this morning," Susan explained. "They only cost two dollars."

Her grandfather looked uncomfortable, and Alex couldn't think of anything to say to make him feel better. He knew the man was proud and didn't like to admit his poverty. Alex also knew John Halvorsen managed to stretch a social security check to take care of himself and a granddaughter with a severe medical problem, an accomplishment well beyond the reach of most people.

"How'd the doctor's appointment go last week?" Alex asked as Susan scampered into the dental chair.

The old man's eyes clouded, and Alex wished he hadn't brought it up.

"Susan's going to have to go back to hospital again," Mr. Halvorsen told him. "That's why I wanted her to see you today. She needs more tests, and then they don't know...."

"That's why Grandpa almost didn't buy me the skates," Susan said. "But I told him I had to get my skating in now if I was going to have to lie around in that stupid old hospital bed again."

"Come on, it's not that bad," Alex said as he pulled on his latex gloves, but from the expression on her grandfather's face, he could tell the old man was worried. Susan had been in and out of the hospital several times for treatment of a heart problem. Alex suspected her doctor might develop a heart problem of his own if he could see her flying down the sidewalk on those roller skates.

He finished with the child quickly, applying some sealant on several teeth with weakened enamel, probably a result of medication she was required to take. As Susan hurried outside, anxious to skate some more, her grandfather pulled three one-dollar bills out of his wallet, which Alex could see was otherwise empty.

"I want to pay you something today, Doc." He held the money toward Alex. "It was going to be more but I let her buy the skates."

Alex felt a lump form in his throat. "That's not necessary," he said, starting to reject the payment. "It's better Susan got the skates."

"No, Doc, you take it. I wouldn't want you to think of us like beggars."

Alex suddenly understood. "Thank you, Mr. Halvorsen," he said, sliding the money into his pocket. "There's no question you pay your own way."

The old man's back straightened slightly and his eyes brightened. Alex knew he'd made the right decision. "When is Susan going into the hospital?" he asked.

"First part of the week," her grandfather answered. "She'll be there awhile this time, the doctor said."

"Wish her luck for me," Alex said.

"She'll need it, Doc."

ALEX WAS STILL IN THE OFFICE an hour later when Ed Meadows, his dental partner, stopped by to pick up his mail.

"What the hell are you doing here so late on a Saturday afternoon? I would think a young fellow like you would be at home getting ready for a hot date tonight."

Alex shrugged his shoulders. "I just didn't get around to setting anything up this weekend." He realized that to Ed, who had been married for thirty years and was nearing retirement, that must seem like a profound waste.

Ed shook his head as he rifled through some letters. "What about your new roommate? Didn't you tell me she's a teacher? Now there's the kind of woman you should get to know better."

If Ed only knew. Alex thought about Gretchen in her bridal costume, then the image faded into Gretchen in her T-shirt and then to Gretchen pressed against him.

"Alex? You with me?"

"Yeah, sure. I was just thinking about my new roommate. She's not your ordinary, everyday teacher type. She's—well . . ."

"You're telling me she's sexy?"

"You could say that."

"No wonder you don't have a date." Ed chuckled on his way out. "You can just go home and hop into the sack with your roommate."

"Not exactly," Alex muttered, which was the very reason he was still in the office. After the way Gretchen had affected him that morning, he wanted to be damned sure she'd already have left for work before he got home.

Once he did leave the office, he stopped for dinner and then killed some time wandering through a bookstore. Even though it was late when he got back to the apartment, he stood outside the door for a long time, listening, before he turned his key in the lock and wheeled his bike inside. What he needed was a hot shower and a quick trip to bed before Gretchen came back.

Peeling off his shirt as he headed for his bedroom, Alex considered moving out of the apartment. Maybe Gretchen had been right. Maybe that would be the best answer. He unbuckled his belt and sat down on his bed to pull off his pants. If he did move out, he could store his things and find a furnished room. His condominium would be finished in a couple of months and he'd be moving then anyway.

Alex stripped off the rest of his clothes and walked naked into the bathroom. Still thinking about his living arrangements, he snapped on the bathroom light and opened the shower curtain. But as he reached out to turn on the water, he stopped and stared. The whole bathtub was full of female underwear. Pink, blue, yellow, every color imaginable. Bras, panties, slips—they were all spread out on a wooden drying rack. Then he saw a note stuck to the vanity mirror and tore it off.

Alex—
Dryer broken. Shower in the morning.

Gretchen

"The hell I will," he muttered as he crumpled the note and dropped it into the wastebasket. He began pulling the silky lingerie off the rack, muttering under his breath as he dropped each wispy garment into the laundry basket. Studying a pair of white panties for a moment, he wondered if Gretchen wore them under that T-shirt. The tiny bit of lace wasn't much, but at least it was something. Feeling his body's response to the memory, he tossed the panties into the basket.

That woman caused him more damned problems, he thought as he carried the laundry basket to Gretchen's bedroom and deposited it in the center of her bed. Not until he put the basket down was he aware that he was stark naked. Gretchen's scent lingered in the room; her possessions were all around him. He looked toward the door, almost expecting to find her standing there. Glancing down, he saw his body's growing anticipation and instantly headed to the bathroom. She sure as hell wasn't going to come home and find him standing naked in her bedroom like that.

Moments later he was in the shower letting the steaming water beat on his back. That was when he made his decision. He wouldn't move out of the apartment. No matter how much underwear she left in the bathroom and no matter how often she bitched about his fish tank, he wasn't going anywhere. Yes, he had to admit she was desirable, and sticking to a strict roommate relationship might be tricky, but he was only going to be living there a couple of months, just until his condominium was ready. Besides, he didn't really see much of Gretchen, and if that changed, he'd just switch to cold showers.

3

THE CARDBOARD SIGN on the grimy window said *Lew's Pawnshop and Loans*. As she pushed open the door and peered inside, Gretchen wondered why she had bothered to wear her good suit. She had a feeling her appearance wasn't going to make much difference.

"I'm in the back. Be with you in a minute," a hoarse voiced called out in answer to the sound of the tarnished brass bell that jangled from the door handle.

Gretchen didn't answer. The place gave her the creeps. She tried to picture Alex, or even Trudy, doing business there. They'd walk out, just like she wanted to do, except she couldn't. The pawnshop was her last hope. As she made her way between the dusty glass cases filled with watches, cameras and jewelry, she wondered how desperate someone must be for money in order to pawn an antique emerald ring or a lustrous strand of matched pearls. As desperate as she was, she decided. If she had anything of value, heirloom or not, she'd gladly pawn it if it meant money for Joyce.

A short, balding man with a cigar in his mouth appeared from behind a set of torn curtains at the rear of the shop. "I'm Lew," he announced. "What can I do for you?"

Gretchen looked him over carefully as he shifted the soggy cigar to the other side of his mouth. His eyes were small and beady, very much like a weasel's. The skin on his face was sallow, and the muscles on one cheek twitched. She decided her best approach was to be brief and honest. There was no point in giving unnecessary information. All she wanted was money—and she wanted it as soon as possible. "I need a loan," she answered firmly.

"Got anything to pawn?" Lew eyed her wristwatch.

"No."

"Got a job?"

Gretchen took a deep breath. "Yes." She didn't elaborate.

"Okay then, come on back to the office."

Lew shoved aside a few overflowing cartons to make room, and Gretchen cautiously followed him through the curtains to the back of the shop. She was more apprehensive with every minute that passed, but she had to go through with it, she told herself. She needed the money. That was all that mattered.

Lew settled himself behind a beat-up, gray metal desk heaped with papers. On one corner a half-empty pot of coffee sitting on an electric hot plate gave off a rancid smell. "Sit down," he grunted, pointing to a folding chair.

Gretchen sat and watched silently while he rummaged through various desk drawers.

"Here it is." He shoved a piece of paper across the littered desk.

Gretchen took the loan application and read it, one side only, nothing written on the back, no small print at the bottom. Not much more than name, address and a reference. She immediately decided to use Trudy's name in the reference space. Then she saw another line that asked for her weekly salary and quickly wrote down five hundred dollars. One week she had made almost that much. "What are the terms of the loan?" she asked.

"Depends on how much you want." Lew shifted his cigar again. The acrid smoke filled the room.

Gretchen swallowed hard. "Five thousand dollars." She gathered up her purse, preparing to leave.

"That'll cost you three hundred a week for six months, due every Wednesday before I close the shop at six. You're late, you pay more."

Three hundred dollars a week! Gretchen's head began to spin as she tried to translate that into performances. She couldn't possibly pay back that much money every week. She had other bills—electricity, the telephone, her share of the rent. And she had to eat something, even if it was cereal and bologna. Then she thought about her sister and all the kids with heart problems who were going to live once Joyce started practicing medicine. She had no choice. She'd work all night, every night, if she had to. Somehow she'd pay the money back. "May I borrow a pen?" she asked evenly.

Twenty minutes later she was standing outside the shop with a check for five thousand dollars in her hand. Her legs were shaking so hard she couldn't take another step. She thought she might laugh, but instead she realized there were tears running down her cheeks. When she reached in her pocket for a tissue her fingers closed over this week's lottery ticket. "Two million dollars," she whispered to herself. She blew her nose and wiped away her tears. Maybe she didn't have a chance of winning the lottery, but that's what everybody thought. Somebody had to win. Why not her?

"DID YOU GET THE MONEY?" Trudy's head poked out of her apartment door.

Gretchen waved the check triumphantly. "All I have to do is deposit it in the bank and send Joyce her tuition check.

"Great, we can take care of it on our way to the thrift shop."

Gretchen hesitated. She hated thrift shops.

"You do remember, don't you?" Trudy prodded. "You promised to help me look for a lamp for my bedroom."

"I remember," Gretchen acknowledged reluctantly, wishing she'd never said she'd do it. "I'll be ready in ten minutes."

"You just missed the hunk," Trudy informed her, as they got into Trudy's car. "He went into the apartment for a few minutes and then he left again."

"You're really keeping close track of him, aren't you?" Gretchen observed.

"Of course not," Trudy said. "I just happened to notice. God, he's good-looking. What's it like to be with him every day?"

"I really wouldn't know," Gretchen replied. "You probably see as much of him as I do. We don't keep the same hours."

"I'll tell you one thing," Trudy said, as she pulled the car into the thrift store parking lot. "If a hunk like that was living in my apartment, I'd change my hours."

"No chance, even if I wanted to," Gretchen answered. "I'm going to be working every minute of my life to make those loan payments."

"Gretchen," Trudy said thoughtfully as she cut the engine on her Toyota, "are you going to be able to pay this loan back?"

A shadow crossed Gretchen's face for an instant. Then she shrugged offhandedly. "I'll just have to pop out of a whole lot of cakes."

"And deliver about a million balloons," Trudy added. "Out of the car. I think I hear my lamp calling me."

Gretchen wrinkled her nose as they went into the thrift shop. Trudy seemed to actually like this place. She said it was a challenge to get something neat for practically nothing. Gretchen felt as if she might gag. The smells were what always got to her the most. Musty, moldy, sweaty— the pungent aroma of poverty that reminded her of her childhood, when most of her clothes had come from the Salvation Army and Goodwill.

Once she had cried all the way home from the store because the only winter jacket that fit her was made of ugly dark blue wool, almost black, and she would rather freeze than wear it. But it had cost only ninety-five cents, as cheap as you could get. She still had that coat packed away in a box as a reminder of how bad things could get. Once she had her teaching job back and Joyce was through medical school, Gretchen planned to burn the coat in a roaring bonfire and then never set foot in a thrift shop again.

"What did I tell you?" Trudy beamed and held up a brass lamp with a shade that was only slightly crooked. "This will be perfect on my nightstand. It would have cost ten times as much if I'd bought it new."

"You really like shopping in here, don't you?" Gretchen asked. She tried to shut out the cacophony of noises assaulting her—the baby crying, the man and his wife arguing about a couch, the beeps of an electronic game and a stereo being tested.

"Of course. It's one of the few ways left to beat the system." Trudy tucked the lamp under her arm and squeezed her way down a narrow aisle between two racks of women's dresses advertised at $2.95 each or two for $5.00. Gretchen followed her, trying not to touch the clothes.

"Most of the stuff in here is junk," Trudy continued as she ran her hand down the line of dresses, "but every so often you come across a really great find."

"You've got your lamp. Can't we just get out of here?" Gretchen asked.

"Gretchen, wait! Look at this." She thrust the lamp into Gretchen's hands and pulled a red dress out of a crush of other clothes on the rack. "I'll bet this is pure silk," Trudy said, holding it up.

Despite her aversion to thrift-store merchandise, Gretchen's eyes widened. The dress was exquisite, with a delicately beaded bodice, softly puffed sleeves and a whisper of a skirt.

Trudy proudly displayed the label, which was from a well-known and very expensive designer. "See, what did I tell you?"

"What size is it?" Gretchen asked, setting the lamp on the floor.

"Size four," Trudy announced, in a disappointed voice. "Wouldn't you know it? No one is that tiny—" She looked hard at Gretchen. "Except you."

"Except me," Gretchen echoed.

"Except you hate clothes from the thrift shop." Trudy kept a firm hold on the dress. "But tell me, Gretchen, just who do you suppose owned this dress before it ended up here?"

Gretchen shook her head. "I have no idea."

"Well, I have," Trudy said, turning the dress around slowly to examine it for flaws. "Somebody with tons of money who spent a fortune for it, wore it once and then ate too much caviar and couldn't fit into it any more."

"I hear you," Gretchen said slowly. "But I don't even need it. Where would I wear a dress like that?" Hesitantly, she took the dress from Trudy and held it in front of her.

"Wow! Gretchen, come over here." She led Gretchen to a cracked mirror propped against a rack of men's suits. "Look at that," Trudy directed. "Just look. It's perfect."

Gretchen took a deep breath as she saw the dress. It *was* perfect, probably the most gorgeous dress she'd ever seen and, as far as she could tell, probably also a perfect fit. "But where would I wear it?" she whispered.

"When you go out with that yuppie hunk you're living with," Trudy answered promptly. "And, I'm telling you, one of these days, you will go out with him."

"You're wrong, Trudy. He's not my type." A tiny flutter stirred inside Gretchen. Alex would love the dress. He would love her in the dress.

"It's always better to be prepared."

"No, really, Trudy. . ." They could go out on the town, to dinner, dancing. She imagined the strains of a string quartet.

"You could tuck it away, just in case."

Gretchen shook her head determinedly, and the string quartet vanished. "Nope," she said, zipping the dress back on a hanger. "On my budget, it's the dress or a lottery ticket this week. I'm going with the lottery ticket. I'd never use the dress anyway."

Immediately Trudy took the dress out of her hands. "Then I'll buy it myself," she announced.

"Why? It doesn't even fit you."

"I know that, but I have a friend who will want to borrow it someday. I'll have it dry-cleaned—just in case."

Rolling her eyes helplessly, Gretchen followed Trudy to the cash register. "There won't be any 'in case.' I am never going to wear that dress." She continued to protest all the way to the car. "You just wasted $2.95."

"Right," Trudy replied. She swung the Toyota onto Wilson Boulevard. "And you're never going out with Alex, either. You've made that perfectly clear, although why you won't go out with him is beyond me. He's the best-looking guy who's been around in months, he's got money—"

"And he *acts* like he's got money," Gretchen finished. "Worse yet, he acts like he's had money all his life."

"How can you tell?"

"I don't know. Just his attitude. Smug. Like he expects life to give him everything. He sure didn't work at a hamburger joint every night all the way through high school."

"Oh, Gretchen, you're too sensitive about your background—"

"You'd be a little sensitive, too, if you'd grown up in a crummy trailer in West Virginia and you'd never eaten a decent meal unless it was paid for with food stamps."

"Come on." Trudy pulled into a parking space in front of their apartment complex. "That's ancient history. You're a college graduate, a teacher, a professional like him—"

"Not like him," Gretchen replied defiantly. "I groveled my way to this point, and my current job is not exactly what you'd call professional." She shoved the car door open and climbed out. As Trudy gathered up her purse, the lamp and the bag with the red silk dress in it, Gretchen stuck her head back in the open door and delivered her parting shot. "You'll be wasting even more money if you take the dress to the cleaners. I'm not going anywhere with Alex Carson. The less I have to do with him, the better off I'll be."

ON SATURDAY, Gretchen put on her complete clown costume—baggy pink and turquoise suit, floppy hat, orange wig, full white makeup and a squeaky red nose. The clown outfit was one of the few costumes Alex hadn't seen yet, she realized as she touched up her makeup. She decided to keep it that way. She waited until she heard Alex go into the bathroom before she emerged from her bedroom and slipped out the front door. The children at the hospital loved Clara the Clown, but Alex would probably think she looked silly. Not that it mattered, she assured herself.

As she headed down the block to where her pink Volkswagen Beetle was parked, the sky was a bright blue, without a cloud in sight, and the weather was unseasonably warm for winter in northern Virginia. Gretchen was in a good mood. She had a letter from Joyce saying the check had come and her tuition was paid, she had a dollar in her pocket for her lottery ticket and for once, she was going to arrive at the hospital on time.

She dumped her oversize, turquoise-colored clown shoes on the passenger's seat and slid behind the wheel of her bug, thinking again how much fun it was to have the bright pink color of the car exactly match her costume. With a wave toward two boys racing by on skateboards, she turned the key and stepped on the gas pedal. The car groaned. Frowning, she tried again. This time, nothing but a series of clicks.

After three more attempts, she jerked the key out of the ignition. The last time the car had sounded like that, a teenager had come along and made some adjustment under the hood to fix the problem. Hopefully, Gretchen looked up and down the street. A grandmotherly sort of woman was walking a poodle, and a young woman was pushing a baby carriage. No prospects there. She could try the gas station but, as usual, she had practically no money. She couldn't skip the hospital visit. Not only was the performance part of her job, but the kids really looked forward to Clara.

Alex. Alex should know something about cars. Most men did. But she hated to admit to him she had a problem she couldn't solve herself. Getting out of the car, Gretchen glanced up and down the empty street again. She needed to get to the hospital, and Alex seemed to be her only answer. He'd been up when she left, she remembered as she hurried along the curving walk through the courtyard that separated the two rows of red brick apartment buildings. He should have had just about enough time to get dressed, which meant he could fix the car right away.

As soon as she stepped inside her apartment, Gretchen could smell the fresh coffee. Her nose led her straight to the kitchen. "Alex, I have a problem with my..." When she saw him, the words stopped. He was wearing nothing but a towel wrapped loosely around his middle. For a moment Gretchen just stared at him, her gaze moving from his lean, muscular legs past the towel to his trim midriff and broad chest with the dark curls, then finally to the shock of damp hair that fell across his forehead. "I guess you just got out of the shower," she said, meeting his eyes. That much was obvious, but it was all she could think of to say.

"That's right." Alex grinned at Gretchen and casually poured himself a cup of coffee. "And I suppose you just came from a circus performance?"

"Not exactly," she answered. "I'm wearing my clown costume because I'm on my way to the hospital and..." Was his towel slipping? She cleared her throat and tried again, forcing herself to look only at his face. "I have a problem," she repeated.

"Is that so?" Alex took a sip of his coffee.

"Yes," Gretchen replied firmly. "My car. It won't start. I guess something's wrong with it."

"If your car won't start there probably is something wrong with it. Is it out of gas?"

"Of course not. The gas gauge was the first thing I checked." She hadn't checked the gas gauge at all, but she had just filled the tank the other day. "I thought you might come take a look at it. Maybe there's something you could do to get it running."

Alex flashed that rakish, sexy grin of his. "I'm not dressed to tear apart a car," he pointed out.

Gretchen refused to look at his towel-clad body. She kept her eyes riveted directly on his. "Neither am I," she answered evenly.

"True." Alex nodded in agreement. He couldn't quite envision her fixing a car in any clothes, but he could picture a lot of other things. She certainly was appealing. Even the baggy clown suit managed to cling in all the right places. Her high, firm breasts were anything but hidden.

"Then you'll help me?" Gretchen asked.

Alex shrugged and set his coffee cup in the sink. Car engines were a mystery to him. He always bought expensive cars, and most of the time they ran well. When they didn't, he took them to a top-notch service station. "I'll give you the name of my mechanic," he volunteered.

Gretchen shook her head. "Nope, no money and no time. I have to be at the hospital in less than an hour."

Alex had a dozen things he was planning to do that afternoon, not the least of which was to play a handball game with his partner. Chauffeuring Gretchen wasn't on the list. Damn! Why did her eyes have to be so big and blue, with those long lashes sweeping her bright red clown cheeks? "I suppose I could give you a lift to the hospital," he said, after finishing his coffee.

"A ride? You won't even look at my car?"

"Nope."

Gretchen sighed in exasperation. "All right," she agreed reluctantly. Men could be so irritating. She watched Alex leave the kitchen, his lean, fluid body moving beneath the towel. Well, maybe all men weren't irritating all the time.

Alex emerged from his bedroom wearing a royal blue warm-up suit and carrying his car keys. As he and Gretchen walked outside, he caught a whiff of the perfume she always wore, that same scent he'd found so unsettling the night he carried her lingerie into her bedroom. He took another look at Gretchen. That scent, and the wisps of blond hair that escaped from under her wig, were about all of her that wasn't obscured by her costume and that heavy makeup. Funny way to spend Saturday afternoons, he thought, playing a clown at a hospital.

"I've got to get my clown shoes out of my car," Gretchen said, stopping abruptly.

As Alex watched, she opened the door of a bilious pink Volkswagen, possibly the ugliest thing he'd ever seen on four wheels. "You call that a car?" he questioned.

"Yes, I do." She slammed the door shut. "And it's very reliable . . . most of the time."

"Why don't you at least get it painted?"

"I just did get it painted," she informed him. "I had it done at a great place that only charges $19.99 if you use a paint color that's in stock. It was pink or mud green."

"I see," Alex said slowly.

"Personally, I rather like it."

Alex didn't answer. There was no accounting for individual tastes. They walked silently down the street to a sleek black Porsche.

"This is your car?" Gretchen gasped. No wonder he'd made fun of her bug if he had an expensive car like this.

"Sure is," Alex answered, unlocking the passenger door so Gretchen could get in. He liked his Porsche and he liked the statement it made, but he sensed it wasn't Gretchen's kind of car. He turned the key and the engine emitted a guttural purr as he pulled away from the curb.

"The money you spent on this car would keep my sister in medical school for a year," Gretchen observed.

"You have a sister in medical school?"

"Yes. She's going to be a pediatric cardiologist. Turn left at the next light and don't change the subject. Anyone who could buy a car like this could afford to stay at the Hilton while he waited for his condominium. Instead you're sharing my apartment, which, I might point out, was not my idea."

"It was your idea to get a new roommate. You just didn't have me in mind."

"You're avoiding the question," she countered. "Just exactly why did you move in with me?"

"I'm short of cash. Honest!" Alex insisted. "I'm buying into the dental practice and I've got payments on my new condominium. For the time being I'm living from week to week."

"You're buying into a dental practice, you own a condominium, you have a Porsche, a microwave, a food processor, a compact disk player and an aquarium full of expensive tropical fish, and you think you're in financial straits? You've got to be kidding! You're nothing but a rich yuppie."

"Now wait a minute," Alex flared. "You're a college graduate, a professional. I think you should include yourself in the yuppie club."

"I'm a destaffed teacher currently making my living from balloons and bachelor parties. My assets include exactly one broken eight-year-old Volkswagen, fourteen dollars in my savings account and—" Gretchen fished in her pocket and brought out a crumpled dollar bill and some change "—except for this dollar that doesn't count, I have exactly two dollars and twenty-seven cents, which has to last me until payday next Wednesday." Gretchen glared at him. "You, Alex, are a rich yuppie. I am practically a street person. Stop in front of that brick building."

Alex followed her direction and glided into a parking space.

"I'll be right back." Gretchen jumped out of the car.

Alex took a deep breath. How could she have so little money? Granted, she wasn't going to get rich working for Shenanigans, but she ought to have more than change to last her until payday. Especially since he had paid all the rent this month.

A few minutes later Gretchen appeared at the car window carrying a huge bunch of multicolored, helium-filled balloons. "Hey, Yuppie, have you got a tire wrench?" she asked.

Bristling, Alex answered tersely. "Probably." Now what was this broad up to? He didn't even want to know. It was easier to just get out of the car, go around to the trunk and locate the wrench. He handed the tool to Gretchen and watched while she eased the balloons into the back of the Porsche and used the wrench to anchor the floating balloons just below the level of the front seats. Then she climbed into the passenger seat. He was still standing by the car trunk when she called to him through the open window.

"Come on, Yuppie, what are you waiting for?"

Alex clenched his teeth. "Nothing, I guess." In reality, he was wondering what the hell he was doing on a perfectly good Saturday afternoon with the rear of his Porsche filled with balloons and the front seat full of a hostile clown.

"Then let's go. The hospital is only a few blocks down on the left, and I want to make one more stop." Gretchen settled back against the soft leather seat and smiled at Alex as he climbed into the car.

"Now where are we going?" he asked.

"To the convenience store at the end of the block."

"We're out of milk?" Alex pulled into a parking space in front of the store.

"Nope, lottery tickets."

"You're broke and you're wasting your money on lottery tickets? I thought you were the poverty-stricken ex-teacher with two dollars and twenty-seven cents to her name."

"I didn't count the lottery money. Besides," Gretchen said as she got out of the car, "you never know when you might win."

Alex was still shaking his head when Gretchen returned to the car stuffing a lottery ticket into her pocket. With a satisfied smile, she put on her clown shoes while Alex drove the remaining few blocks.

As they pulled into the circular drive at the main entrance to the hospital, Alex remembered that Susan's grandfather had said she was going to be admitted early in the week. He checked his watch. Not enough time to stop by and see her.

"Thanks for the ride, Yuppie," Gretchen said, as she climbed awkwardly out of the Porsche and maneuvered her floppy turquoise feet to the sidewalk.

"Wait a minute." Alex swallowed his irritation as he got out of the car. "You go to the hospital to entertain kids, right?"

"Basically."

"Then you can do me a favor. Look up a little girl named Susan Halvorsen and give her a red balloon. Tell her it's from Dr. Carson."

Gretchen looked at him curiously. "Is she a daughter of one of your friends?"

"No, she's a patient of mine. Nice kid. She's got a heart problem."

Alex couldn't see Gretchen's expression behind the clown makeup as he unwound the balloons from the tire wrench and handed them to her. Nor did he catch the hesitation in her voice when she said, "Sure, I'll go to see her."

"How will you get home?" he asked.

"Oh, I don't know. I'll figure something out."

Alex watched Gretchen, usually so graceful, lumber through the hospital doors. Big blue eyes or not, she was a bundle of contradictions. He gunned the motor of his car and pulled away from the curb. Damned if he cared how she got home. If necessary, she could walk back to the apartment. He glanced at the threatening gray sky. So, she could walk in the rain. She'd survive. He had a handball game waiting for him—a nice, yuppie handball game.

4

HOLDING THE HELIUM BALLOONS close to her body so they wouldn't be too cumbersome, Gretchen pushed open the door to the children's ward and nearly collided with a nurse.

"Oops, sorry, my big feet are always getting in the way." She slapped her floppy turquoise shoes on the linoleum floor.

"That's okay, Clara," replied the nurse, whom Gretchen recognized as a friend of Trudy's. "We're always glad to see you, big feet or not."

"Is there anyone special I should visit after my show is over?"

The nurse thought for a moment. "Yes, Joey is still in traction in Room 7, and there's a new patient, a seven-year-old with a heart problem, in 4-B. Her name is Susan."

Gretchen froze for a second. Susan, the little girl Alex wanted her to visit. The one with a heart problem. A rush of memories surged inside her, and twelve years melted away as though they had never existed. She remembered the months of hoping with her little sister, Nancy, who'd been home briefly and then back to the hospital again. For a long time she'd thought Nancy would get better. But she never had. And then one day she was gone. The memories were vivid, too vivid.

Suddenly Gretchen wanted to turn around and leave the hospital and never come back. Instead, she gave the nurse her best Clara the Clown smile along with the expected response. "I'll be sure not to miss Joey. . . or Susan."

"Great, see you later." The nurse bustled into the linen room.

Gretchen lumbered down the corridor toward the playroom. The pale green walls of the ward, although decorated with whimsical murals, seemed to close in on her. When an orderly rolled a tall food cart past the nurse's station, she could hear the clanking of metal and smell the steamy, overcooked food all the way down the hall. The noise from the cart was punctuated several times by monotone pagings over the public address system. From somewhere came the thin wail of a child in pain.

Gretchen closed her eyes, trying to shut out all the sights and sounds. But even with her eyes closed the smell of disinfectant rose up from the floor and burned her nostrils. She leaned against the cold tile wall, trying not to remember. She had avoided hospitals for years, ever since Nancy died, until she had started working for Shenanigans, and visiting the hospital was part of the job.

Wearing her clown costume, Gretchen had found each visit easier than the last . . . until today. She took a deep breath and stood up very straight. If Gretchen couldn't handle visiting sick children, Clara the Clown could, she thought determinedly. Clara could even handle the little girl with the heart problem. With a squeak of her nose, she poked her head into the playroom, waiting until the giggles told her Clara had been noticed. Then she somersaulted into the room and began her routine.

An hour later, after another successful show, she lumbered down the hall and slipped into Joey's room, but the little boy was sleeping. She tied a bright yellow balloon to his bed rail to let him know Clara had been by for a visit. Holding the last remaining balloon, a red one for Susan, she peeked inside the open door of Room 4-B and squeaked her nose.

"A clown!" a piping voice squealed. "You brought me a red balloon!"

"Hi there, Susie Q. I'm Clara." Gretchen went over to the side of the bed and tied the balloon to the rail. "This balloon comes from a very special friend of yours."

"From Gramps?" Susan asked.

"No, from Dr. Carson," Gretchen told her. "He said it had to be red."

"I like Dr. Carson," Susan replied, tugging at the balloon string. "I didn't know he knew any clowns. Do you like him, too?"

"Yes, I . . . I do like Dr. Carson," Gretchen said. The realization was very unsettling.

Gretchen flashed her best clown smile at the pigtailed little girl who was propped up on several pillows. Susan's face was pale, with a scattering of freckles across her nose, but her eyes were alert and happy. Gretchen swallowed hard, almost seeing Nancy's big brown eyes looking up at her. "How are you doing today?" she asked gently.

Susan hugged her teddy bear. "Not so good. The nurses won't let me roller skate in the hall, and Gramps brought my roller skates and everything. I got them just last week, and I'm a really good roller skater."

Gretchen looked down at the roller skates and then back at Susan. A heart monitor on a stand next to the bed hummed as it traced her heart rhythms on a strip of paper. Susan could barely sit up, much less roller skate, even if roller skating was allowed in the hospital.

"You'd really like to skate, wouldn't you?" Gretchen said sympathetically.

"Yes," Susan replied. "I was just starting to figure out how to go superfast when I had to come back to the hospital again."

Gretchen felt her eyes stinging with tears she couldn't shed. Clowns don't cry, she silently reminded herself. She knew that Susan, with her heart problem, might never be well enough to roller skate again. Or ride a bike. Or climb a tree. Or do anything that healthy kids simply take for granted. That was what had happened to her sister. On Nancy's last Christmas there had been a red two-wheeler waiting for her next to the tree. She had wanted to go outside and ride it immediately, and everyone had laughed because there was a foot of snow on the ground. But Nancy had been only eight years old and much too excited to remember she couldn't ride a bike in the snow. She never did get to ride the bike. By the time the snow melted Nancy had died.

Gretchen pushed the roller skates under the bed, out of sight. "These will be here when you're ready to use them," she promised. "In the meantime, how about playing a game?"

"Do clowns play games?" Susan asked skeptically.

"Yes," Gretchen answered firmly. "Clowns play all kinds of games."

Susan's eyes brightened. "Then let's play checkers."

Gretchen laid the checker board out on the tray table. This was going to be tough. Taking a deep breath, she dumped the checkers on the board. "Okay, Susie Q," she said with a big clown smile. "Red or black?"

ALEX PACED AROUND the hospital lobby, picked up a magazine, tossed it on the end table and paced some more. He'd tried to get into the pediatric ward to see Susan, but visiting hours were over. Actually, he'd known he was too late before he'd asked, just as he knew the real reason he'd come to the hospital was to give Gretchen a ride home.

He had a dozen reasons for deciding to help her out. It was raining. She had no money for the bus. It was almost three miles to the apartment. But they were still excuses. Alex knew that, too. He slumped down on a nondescript gray chair and stared out the window at the rain running down the glass. He had to be losing his mind. He didn't need to be there. Gretchen was a big girl, and she could take care of herself. Hell, he'd even brought her an umbrella.

The elevator light blinked and Alex looked expectantly across the crowded lobby. He heard the laughter and watched as several people moved aside to let the clown through. Still playing the role, Gretchen squeaked her nose and paused to talk to a little boy with a cast on his arm. Alex walked toward her, wondering what he was going to say.

"Hi, there," he began.

Gretchen looked up at him. "Hello," she said. There wasn't a trace of emotion in her voice.

"I came to give you a ride home."

No response. Alex had expected at least a protest. She had certainly been feisty a few hours ago. He studied Gretchen carefully for a moment. Her eyes, usually such a vibrant blue, were clouded and distant. Her body was limp. Overall, she appeared absolutely drained. Pushing open the heavy glass doors at the hospital's main entrance, he guided her outside. "I brought an umbrella because it's raining," he said unnecessarily. "Why don't you wait here while I get the car?"

Gretchen nodded.

A few minutes later Alex pulled the Porsche up to the curb and Gretchen slid into the passenger seat. By the time he turned onto Wilson Boulevard she had removed her red nose and the hat and wig, freeing her blond hair which curled softly around her face. But she still hadn't spoken. The only sound inside the car was the swishing of the windshield wipers. Alex couldn't figure out what was wrong. If Gretchen was mad at him, why didn't she say so? Yet she seemed more withdrawn than angry. Finally he asked conversationally, "Was the pediatric ward full today?"

"Yes, there were some new children."

Well, at least she had answered. "Is that right?" he replied.

Gretchen stared out the window. "I saw Susan, the little girl you wanted me to visit. I gave her the red balloon."

"Oh..."

"She has big brown eyes like my little sister."

"The one who's in medical school now?"

Gretchen shook her head. "No, that's Joyce. I'm talking about my younger sister, Nancy."

Again the silence, but something inside told Alex to wait. The wiper blades continued their rhythmic swishing across the windshield. After several minutes Gretchen spoke again.

"Nancy died when I was fifteen." She said the words with no trace of emotion.

Twelve years ago, Alex thought. A long time. And yet Gretchen was still hurting. He pulled the car into a parking place on the street in front of the apartment complex and turned off the motor. For a few minutes they sat quietly. Alex listened to the rain beating a steady pattern on the roof and watched Gretchen. She was staring out the window, not seeing anything. The heavy rain washed down the windshield, closing them off from the world.

"How did Nancy die?" he asked gently.

Gretchen turned and looked into his eyes. They were dark brown, soft and understanding. "Nancy died of a congenital heart problem," she answered in a low voice. "She was sick for a long time, but we always kept hoping...."

No wonder Gretchen was so withdrawn. Now the pieces were beginning to fit together. "Today must have been hard for you," he said.

Gretchen nodded. "Oh, Alex," she burst out suddenly, "why does a child have to die?" Tears began to slip down her cheeks, making rivulets in the white clown makeup. "I'm sorry," she whispered. "I never cry. I'm the one who is always in control, who always takes care of everyone else. I never come apart."

"It's all right," Alex said quietly. He took her hands and waited while she cried softly for a few minutes more. She seemed very fragile, very vulnerable. Yet what she said about always taking care of everybody else.... When her tears subsided he handed her his handkerchief. "Gretchen," he began thoughtfully, "are you helping to keep your sister in medical school?"

"Yes." She wiped her eyes and blew her nose. "Someday she'll be able to help other children like Nancy...." She looked away as her voice broke again.

"I understand." And much more than she'd told him. Now he knew why Gretchen worked such long hours and why she never had any money. She was sacrificing beyond anything a normal woman realistically had a right to expect of herself. Suddenly he was embarrassed about the substantial trust fund that had put him through college and dental school. For one of the few times in his life he was at a loss for words.

"Thanks for listening, Yuppie," Gretchen said in a shaky voice. She gripped Alex's hands very tightly and gave him a tentative smile.

"Anytime," Alex promised, getting out of the car. This time when she called him "yuppie," the label hadn't grated. He wasn't sure why.

Gretchen watched him walk around the car, his stride confident. When he helped her get out, his hands were warm and strong.

"Watch your feet—uh, shoes, or whatever—in the puddles," he cautioned.

Gretchen bent down and pulled off the big turquoise shoes while he shielded her from the rain with his umbrella. She stuffed the floppy shoes in the bag with her hat, wig and nose and walked under the umbrella beside Alex toward the apartment.

"You really were nice to come pick me up," she told him. She wasn't sure what she'd have done in costume, in the rain, if he hadn't been there. He could be considerate sometimes.

"No problem. What are you going to do about your car?"

"Get it fixed, I guess," Gretchen answered. "Do you know anyplace cheap?"

Alex shook his head. He wished he did, and he wished he knew enough about cars that he could do it for her. That was really the only thing she'd ever asked of him. He opened the apartment door for her, struggling with a strange mixture of feelings. This woman he'd pegged initially as a flaky broad in a sequined costume was turning out to have more facets than he'd expected. He realized he was beginning to like her.

Once inside the apartment, Gretchen dropped her bag in the closet. As she walked toward her bedroom, she reached for the zipper at the back of her rain-splattered clown suit.

"Here, let me help you," Alex offered.

As he came up behind her, Gretchen hesitated. She could manage the long zipper just fine by herself. She did it all the time. But it seemed so natural to let Alex do it. Then his fingers were on the back of her neck and the zipper crept slowly down the length of her body. She shivered at every touch of his hands.

"Are you cold?"

"Not really," she replied. "It's just that the clown suit is a little damp from the rain." Maybe that was part of it, she tried to tell herself, but the feelings were all wrong.

"You'd better get into some dry clothes," Alex suggested. "We don't need a clown with a cold."

Gretchen slipped her arms out of the baggy clown costume, let it drop to her feet and stepped out of it.

She heard Alex catch his breath and suddenly she felt next to naked. She was wearing a black leotard, as she always did under the clown costume. But she felt as if she was wearing nothing at all. She didn't have to look around to know he was watching her every movement. After that morning in the kitchen when the sparks flew between them, she didn't have to ask what he was looking at. She wasn't sure what to do about it. She turned and her eyes found his, dark and intense. She wasn't sure she wanted to do anything about it. Were the signals she was sending him as blatant as the ones she was getting from him?

"Gretchen," he began in a husky voice. The sight of her in the body-molding black leotard was almost more than he could handle. The fabric clung to every curve of her body. Especially her breasts. Rounded and firm with the nipples erect—he knew damned well she wasn't wearing a bra, and probably no panties, either. Even that wispy stuff she called underwear would have left ridges under the tight leotard. And there were definitely no ridges anywhere that didn't belong. He felt his body tighten, the same reaction he got every time he saw her in one of these scanty outfits.

"Gretchen," he started again, then stopped. What the hell was he going to say? How about hopping into bed for some late afternoon sex? That was rather blunt.

"Yes?" She knew exactly what he wanted. Sex. Her response to him seemed to split apart. Of course she wouldn't have sex with him, the logical part of her mind said. Why not, another voice inside whispered. It was a dark, chilly day and he was warm and male and available. She felt the heat rising inside. Her palms grew moist. She heard the rain beat a pulsing, steady rhythm against the window. Taking a step toward him, she put her hand on his chest and smoothed away a wrinkle in his sweatshirt. "Yes, Alex?"

She had answered without him having to ask. He hadn't expected her to be so willing. Now all he had to do was get rid of the clown face. As desirable as the rest of her body was, he wasn't prepared to make love to a clown. "I want to kiss you, Gretchen," he told her, touching her hair and moving closer to her. "But—your makeup?"

"Oh!" She put both hands to her cheeks, still gritty white. "I forgot." How could he be attracted to her at all with the face of a clown? "I've got a bottle of baby oil in the bedroom." Reluctantly, she turned away from him. "It'll just take me a minute."

Alex followed her into the bedroom, and once she had located the bottle of baby oil and some old cotton washcloths, he sat her firmly on the bed. "I'll do it," he said.

Gretchen dampened one of the washcloths with baby oil and handed it to him. Then she closed her eyes and waited. The oil was cool and slippery against her skin as he wiped her face, beginning with her forehead and moving slowly downward.

"I'm beginning to find the real you under all this," he said as he stroked. "Did you know you have perfect eyebrows?" He traced one brow with the tip of his finger. "And a very nice nose?" He drew the soft washcloth slowly down each side of her nose.

"Mmm." Gretchen sighed.

"And lovely, rounded cheeks." His hand moved in leisurely circles, first on one side of her face and then the other.

Gretchen sighed again. She'd never known removing makeup could be such a sensuous experience.

"But I especially like your mouth. Perfectly bowed lips, pouting just enough."

Alex leaned closer to her and oiled her lips with his fingers, rimming them round and round as he softened the red clown paint. Then, with a dry cloth, he wiped away the last of the makeup and the oil with it. Slowly she opened her eyes and gazed into his. They were dark and intense as he pulled her to him.

His lips touched hers, and a swirl of sensation shot through her. The only other time he had kissed her had been that morning in the kitchen, but she had been so startled that she scarcely remembered how it felt. But this time was different. She would remember this. His lips were hot and wet and tasted like a rich burgundy wine. Tiny tremors ran through her body, leaving warm pulsing places in their wake. She pressed against him, shuddering as he outlined her lips with the tip of his tongue. He smelled very musky, very male. She felt his fingers on her bare shoulder as he eased away the edge of her leotard and pushed her back on the bed. She held her breath, expecting to feel his hands next, spreading their warmth to her breasts that ached unbearably for his touch.

But his hands didn't move. She waited, feeling his breath against her cheek. He was barely touching her at all. After a moment she opened her eyes and found him studying her. When she leaned toward him, her body stinging with sensation, he pulled away.

"Why are you doing this, Gretchen?" he asked her. Something was happening inside him, something he couldn't quite figure out. He'd been impatient at the beginning because he'd wanted her the way any man would want a woman who looked like Gretchen, except the makeup had been in the way. But as he had exposed the woman beneath the clown face, touching her inch by inch, he'd seen her differently. And he'd begun to feel differently. "I think I hardly know you," he murmured.

Gretchen stared at him. She'd been ready, quivering at his slightest touch, willing to have him take her away from all her problems for a little while. And now he was muttering about not knowing her. "You seem to have changed direction rather abruptly." She moved away from him, not caring that the statement sounded like an accusation.

"I guess I did." Alex stood up. What the hell was he doing? She was right there, ready for the taking, and he was walking away. He turned and took her hand. The instant he touched her he felt the fire between them. Damn, he still wanted her too much to care about anything else.

But this time Gretchen pulled away and stood up, facing him squarely. Frustrated with desire, she shook her head. "If you think I'm some toy to play with, you can think again."

Alex shoved his hands in his pockets. "It's not like that, Gretchen." He wished he could explain what it was like, but he didn't know himself. All he knew was that a quick roll in the hay had lost its appeal while the woman he was going to do it with seemed more desirable than ever. His mind searched for a diversion. "Let's do something else," he suggested, having a hard time believing it was Alex Carson saying those words. "It's almost dinnertime. You want to go out?"

"I have to work tonight." Her tone was cold.

"Then how about I go pick up some Chinese take-out? That'll only take a few minutes."

She was ready to tell him no, no to anything he suggested. She was angry. She gazed at him for a long moment, watching his jaw tighten and release. Then from somewhere inside her that shred of reason she'd ignored at the beginning resurfaced. If she'd wanted to be perfectly candid, which she didn't, she'd have had to admit that sex with Alex hadn't really been what she'd been after. Although she'd been more than willing.

But what she'd really wanted was an escape, a total and absolute escape from the memories of her little sister's death, from the enormous sadness she'd felt when she visited Susan in the hospital. Alex had offered her a way out, if only for a little while, and she'd been ready to take it. Now she was glad she hadn't.

"I guess Chinese take-out would be a good idea," she said, managing a smile. "I'll get ready for work while you go pick it up." But once he'd left, she found herself wandering aimlessly, twice losing her hairbrush, unable to concentrate on what she was doing. When Alex came back with dinner, she was barely ready. As they ate cashew chicken and rice, he talked about the rain and she talked about the party where she had to perform that evening.

Not until after she'd put on her coat did she turn and look him in the eye. "Alex, about what happened . . ." He glanced up at her from the couch where they'd sat to eat dinner, and she knew he understood.

"What did happen?" he asked slowly.

"Well, we . . . I mean I . . ."

Smiling gently as she tripped over the words, he stood up and reached out to touch her shoulder. "Maybe nothing happened, Gretchen."

"Maybe you're right," she answered slowly.

She turned, and he let her go. She didn't believe it, and she had a feeling he didn't, either.

ALEX WOULD HAVE BEEN Gretchen's number-one all-consuming problem if she hadn't also had to deal with money. Despite all the extra hours of work, she barely had enough cash left for food once she had made the first loan payment to Lew. After a lengthy deliberation in which she considered how little sleep she could get and still function, she added a belly-dance act to her routine and tried to fit in as many extra performances as possible.

Her broken car was another problem. For more than a week she had been using public transportation or bumming rides to work. Finally she'd had the pink bug towed to a service station. The diagnosis wasn't good.

"You got a bad starter, lady, and it's killed the battery, too."

Gretchen pulled her coat more closely around her sheer, green harem pants and gold-spangled bra top. "Just tell me how much this is going to cost," she directed the mechanic.

"Let's see," he muttered as he scrawled on the work order. "Ninety-two fifty for a starter, sixty dollars for the battery plus labor."

Gretchen held her breath while he added up the figures.

"Comes to two hundred forty dollars, plus tax, roughly. Oh, yeah, I almost forgot the towing charge. Twenty-five dollars, plus five dollars a mile after the first two miles. Three extra miles. . . ." He muttered to himself again.

"Two hundred eighty dollars," Gretchen said in a weak voice. Almost the same amount as the loan payment.

"You want me to go ahead and fix it?"

There really wasn't any choice. Without the car it was almost impossible to get to work. She'd already turned down two good jobs because they weren't on the bus or metro line and she couldn't get a ride. If she couldn't work she couldn't pay her bills. Worse yet, she couldn't make the loan payments. She considered Lew's weasel eyes. She had to have her car. "How soon can you have it ready?" she asked.

"Tomorrow morning okay?"

Gretchen nodded. "I'll pick it up on my way to work." If I can figure out how to pay for it, she thought.

She spent the next forty minutes adding and subtracting figures while she endured the lurching bus that carried her to her first performance. The options were nonexistent. Either she paid for the car repairs or she made the second payment on the loan. She couldn't do both.

When she came home from work, she got off the bus two stops before her own—despite the fact that it was nearly three in the morning and very cold—and dropped a nice note into the mail slot of the pawnshop explaining her predicament with the broken car and telling Lew she was going to skip the second payment. As an afterthought she had added a postscript telling him to just tack the payment on at the end. Pleased with her solution, and doubly pleased because she managed to deliver the note two days before the payment was actually due, she fell exhausted into bed and slept like a rock.

ALEX WRESTLED with his feelings about Gretchen all week. Several evenings he waited up for her until midnight hoping they'd at least have a few minutes to talk. But it seemed all she did was work. That night he *didn't* want her to come home. He assumed she wouldn't, but he had to be sure. After some consideration he stuck a note on the bathroom mirror:

Gretchen—
Do you have plans for Friday night?

A.

Gretchen found the note very late at night as she stood wearily in front of the bathroom mirror and reached for her toothbrush. Surprised, she read the note three times before she finally concluded Alex was asking her for a date. "Damn," she sputtered to herself. She had one of the biggest bachelor parties of the year booked for Friday night. There was no way she could get out of it, and even if there had been, she couldn't afford to lose the money. This particular gig was going to pay well, and she might even get a few good-sized tips.

"Damn," she sputtered again. She hadn't seen Alex for days. All she'd done was work, for hours on end, until one job blurred into another. She had changed from a French maid to a bride to a clown to a harem dancer so often that she was sure she was going to pop out of the wedding cake as Clara the Clown. Some sexy routine that would be. She really would like to spend an evening with Alex. The memory of his lips on hers was vivid and very pleasant. When she thought about him, which was often, her focus was more and more on Alex the man instead of Alex the yuppie.

Gretchen crumpled the note and pitched it in the waste-basket. The sticky memo she left in its place on the mirror was brief and to the point:

Alex—
Terribly sorry. I have to work tonight.

                                                            G.

5

"GRETCHEN, I'VE GOT TO TALK to you!" Trudy burst into the apartment on Friday just as Gretchen was finishing her lunch. "I've been trying to catch you for two days."

"Sorry, Trudy, I've been working a lot lately." Gretchen led her neighbor into the kitchen.

"It's a good thing you haven't been here." Clutching her ever-present coffee mug, Trudy sat down at the table across from Gretchen. "There's been a man hanging around a lot asking for you."

"A man?" Gretchen took a large bite of her bologna sandwich. One of the other performers had a problem with a man following her home from a party and then hanging around and bothering her. But if that's what it was, she could handle it. "What did he look like?"

"He was kind of greasy looking," Trudy said. "I really had a bad feeling about him, and I didn't like the way he talked."

"What did he say?"

"First he wanted to know if I'd seen you, and of course I said no because that was true. I hadn't seen you. And then he wanted to know if you lived here."

Gretchen frowned. "What did you tell him?"

"I wasn't sure what to do so I asked him why he wanted to know." Trudy stood up to get the ashtray Gretchen kept for her in the kitchen drawer and lit a cigarette. "He said he had some business with you and if I saw you, I was to tell you Lew was looking for you."

Gretchen almost choked on her milk. "His name was Lew?"

Trudy nodded.

A cold chill settled around Gretchen. "Was this man short, kind of round and bald? And chewing a cigar?"

"That's the one," Trudy said, "and come to think of it he did have a cigar. Do you know him?"

Gretchen stood up slowly and carried her dishes to the sink. "Unfortunately, yes, I do. He's the man from the loan company."

"Oh, Gretchen, no." Trudy ground out her cigarette. "I wish I'd never mentioned the place. What is he doing bothering you here?"

"It's not your fault, Trudy. I'm the one who made the mess."

"What do you mean?"

"I couldn't make the second payment on the loan because I had to get my car fixed, and so I wrote Lew a really nice note explaining the problem." She turned around and leaned against the counter. "Maybe it would help if I called him?" she suggested.

Trudy shook her head. "From the looks of him, all that guy understands is money. You're better off avoiding him till you have some. How long do you think it will take?"

"I should have enough for next week's payment," Gretchen said. "I'm signed up for so many jobs this weekend that it makes my head spin to think about them." She paced the kitchen. "Everything would have been fine without the bill for the stupid car."

"So, just stay out of his way till you can pay him," Trudy advised. "If he comes back again, I'll tell him I think you moved. And remember, I've still got the two hundred dollars if you're crunched."

"Thanks, Trudy, but I won't be that crunched." Gretchen gathered up her costume bag and her purse from the kitchen counter. "I guess I ought to get going if I'm going to earn all this money."

As she and Trudy left the apartment, Gretchen had a disturbing thought. "Trudy, you don't think he's talked to Alex, do you?" She didn't care if Trudy knew what she'd done. Trudy understood. But she didn't want Alex in on it. Someone with his background wouldn't understand at all. People with money never understood the problems of people who had no money.

Trudy shrugged. "I suppose he might have talked to Alex. There's no way of knowing—unless you ask Alex."

"No chance!" Gretchen replied. "He'd think I was a real airhead to get into a mess like this."

"Not if he knew why you did it," Trudy argued.

"Even then."

"Does it matter?" Trudy asked, looking squarely at Gretchen.

"No . . . yes . . . of course not," Gretchen stammered. "I have to go or I'll be late for work."

GRETCHEN HAD THREE JOBS that afternoon, all of them requiring her French maid costume, a lacy white apron over a short black satin dress that just covered the tops of her net stockings. The first job, a simple delivery of a bouquet of happy birthday balloons, was a disaster. After Gretchen spent nearly an hour locating the address, the recipient wasn't home.

"Why does this always happen to me?" she muttered to no one in particular. Inside, she knew exactly why. Instead of paying attention to where she was going, she'd managed to get lost twice because she'd been thinking about Alex and wishing she could spend the evening with him. At the rate things were going, she was never going to see him. Some day his condominium would be finished and she'd find a note on the mirror saying he'd enjoyed knowing her.

"Stop being stupid," she lectured herself. Working day and night was the only way she was going to pay off the loan. She'd already decided that. And as far as Alex was concerned, thinking about him at all was ridiculous. They were from two different worlds. She forced herself to focus on her next two jobs, a retirement party and an anniversary.

When she left the anniversary celebration she headed for a pay phone to call the Shenanigans office and get her evening schedule. As she opened her change purse to take out a quarter, she saw her lottery ticket tucked inside. The jackpot was up to $2.2 million. That would be enough happiness to last a lifetime. Gretchen took out the ticket and traced each number individually before returning it to her change purse and snapping it shut. She could always dream.

The receptionist at the office put her on hold for several minutes before giving her the good news. The only party scheduled for that evening had been canceled because the bridegroom had suddenly left for Canada without the bride.

Gretchen whooped for joy. She'd still get paid in full because the cancellation came so late, and she'd have her first free Friday night in weeks. Not only that, but tonight was the night Alex had asked her for a date. Well, sort of asked her, but it amounted to the same thing. She had a quarter in her hand, ready to call him with the good news, when she changed her mind. It would be more fun to surprise him.

She thought about him all the way home. She didn't have enough money to go out to dinner, but she did have five dollars. If she and Alex split the cost, they could broil a steak at home and then go to one of the cut-rate movies out in Falls Church. Or, if he offered to pay, they could go to a first-run movie. Her step was light as she hurried up the stairs. She hadn't even considered the other possibility. Alex might already have made plans for them. After all, he was the one who had asked her out. He would be so surprised and so pleased she was able to go.

Gretchen had taken her key out of her purse and was ready to unlock the door when she heard voices inside the apartment. She stopped, listening. Definitely two voices. She recognized Alex's right away. But the other voice was *female*.

Gretchen's spirits fell with a thud. She was too late. Alex had a woman with him. When he'd found out she was working, he'd apparently invited someone else, and he certainly hadn't wasted any time doing it. So much for eating steaks and going to a movie. So much for her free Friday evening that was to have been so much fun.

Leaning nearer the door, she tried to make out their words, but their voices were too soft. She started to insert her key in the lock, then stopped. What were they doing in there? After all, Alex didn't expect her home till late, and he would have assumed he had the apartment all to himself. Surely they weren't doing *that*. Gretchen shifted from one foot to the other as she tried to assess the little noises audible through the door. None sounded familiar. Besides, if they were doing what she thought, they should be in the bedroom where she wouldn't have been able to hear them at all. Of course they wouldn't necessarily have to be in the bedroom. . . .

Gretchen dropped her key in the pocket of her apron and rapped sharply on the door. Now she had to knock on her own door to get into her own apartment because her roommate was doing who knew what with some woman, probably on *her* sofa!

The door opened almost immediately and Alex appeared, dressed in a blue patterned sweater and a pair of slacks. The horrified look on his face clearly said he was not the least bit happy to see her. Well, she wasn't happy to see him right then, either.

"Gretchen," he hissed. "What are you doing here?"

"This is my apartment! I live here, remember, Yuppie?" She started inside, but he blocked the door.

"Quiet!" he ordered in a loud whisper.

"Do you have company, Alex?" called a female voice from the kitchen. Gretchen tried to look over Alex's shoulder but couldn't see anyone.

"For God's sake, Gretchen, pretend you don't live here!" Alex exclaimed in a loud whisper. "I'll explain later."

Gretchen was about to tell him she didn't care about what he was doing—which wasn't true—and that she was mad as hell about having to knock on the door of her own apartment—which was true—when Alex stepped back from the doorway. Behind him stood a tall, fashionably dressed woman in a dusty-pink wool dress, her gray hair brushed softly back from her face. She was wearing a single string of pearls, matching earrings and diamond rings on both hands. All in all, she struck Gretchen as the classic picture of understated elegance.

"Mother, I'd like you to meet my neighbor, Gretchen Bauer," Alex said stiffly. "Gretchen, this is my mother."

Gretchen was so dumbfounded that she was totally unable to respond. A strange mixture of amazement, relief and disbelief swept through her. He didn't have a date and he hadn't been doing any of the things she'd imagined while she stood outside the door. She forced a weak smile. So this was Alex's mother. First his aquarium, then his bike, and now his mother.

"How nice to meet you, Gretchen," the woman was saying, her eyes fixed on Gretchen's skimpy French maid outfit.

Alex obviously caught his mother's look, too. "Gretchen is . . . ah . . . a performer," he explained. "She's here to . . . a . . . borrow a cup of sugar. You wait here, Gretchen, and I'll get it for you." He hurried toward the kitchen.

A cup of sugar? He was really desperate. Obviously he didn't want his mother to know they were living together, however innocent the circumstances. She could understand why. The woman certainly looked formidable.

"Exactly what kind of performer are you?" Alex's mother asked.

Gretchen realized his mother was still staring at her costume. "I'm, well . . ." Shenanigans was always a little hard to explain. Besides, this woman didn't look like the type who would be able to understand her job no matter how she described it. "I do various kinds of acts," Gretchen said finally.

"How . . . interesting," Alex's mother answered, obviously skeptical.

Just then Alex came back into the living room lugging a five-pound sack of sugar. Gretchen clapped her hand over her mouth to keep from laughing. The sight of Alex so strung out because of his mother was almost more than Gretchen could stand. She grinned wickedly. "You don't have to give me the whole bag of sugar," she said in an innocent voice. "You never know when you might want to bake a cake."

Alex glared at her. "I won't be needing sugar tonight." He shoved the five-pound sack into her arms. "Just take the whole thing."

He took a step forward and Gretchen knew he was trying to hustle her out of the door. She leaned around him. "So nice to meet you, Mrs. Carson," she said sweetly. "I hope we'll see each other again."

Alex's mother only nodded.

"You get exactly one hour, Yuppie," Gretchen hissed as she backed out into the hall. "Then I'm coming back and..."

"Thanks," he whispered, quickly closing the door.

Once the door was shut, even the small pleasure of needling Alex was gone. Gretchen walked slowly downstairs, wondering how to kill an hour wearing a French maid's costume and carrying a five-pound bag of sugar. To make matters worse, a light, misty rain had started falling. Gretchen buttoned her coat and pulled the collar snugly around her neck, wishing she had an umbrella.

It was already dark as she started down the sidewalk that split the apartment complex. Every fifty feet or so, small gas lights glowed in the deserted courtyard, their light blurred by the mist. She walked slowly, listening to the staccato sound of her high heels clicking against the bricks. Nearing the end of the sidewalk, she paused and tried to decide what to do next. For a split second she thought she heard the muffled sound of footsteps behind her. Then the sound stopped. Gretchen started walking again, faster this time, then stopped abruptly to listen. Again she heard the footsteps and knew instinctively that she was being followed. She quickly turned the corner and ducked behind a row of tall, wet bushes alongside the building. She waited, barely breathing.

Moments later, a man with a large umbrella appeared at the end of the sidewalk. The gas light reflected off his bald head as he looked up and down Wilson Boulevard and scanned the bushes along both sides of the building. Then he turned, and the light crossed his face. Gretchen moved deeper into the shadows, peering out around the bush. It was Lew from the pawnshop, and he'd come for his money.

Taking a deep breath, she tried to think. He wouldn't hurt her. She was sure of that, or at least almost sure. What he wanted was the money, and she didn't have it. Not yet. But she'd only missed one payment and that was for the car so she could work and make the other payments. She should just walk right out there and explain. Cowering behind a bush in the rain was stupid.

But Gretchen didn't move. Maybe it wasn't necessary to tell him at night, she thought. There was no reason she couldn't wait until daylight. That would be better. She stood perfectly still and watched Lew for several minutes. A car pulled away from the curb about halfway down the block and he shrugged his shoulders and crossed the street. Finally, he climbed into a black Corvette and drove away, but Gretchen stayed where she was until the car's tail-lights disappeared.

She should have just confronted him, she told herself, laughing shakily as she emerged from behind the bush and shook the rain from her hair. All she'd done was miss one loan payment. Shifting the wet bag of sugar to her other arm, she crossed the street toward a fast-food restaurant. Maybe a hamburger and a cup of coffee would help her regain her equilibrium.

So far, the evening was a disaster, she thought as she sat down at a corner table. She'd cowered behind a dripping bush, been hustled out of her own apartment as if she was an intruder, and now she was stuck with a hamburger that resembled greasy cardboard. If it weren't for Alex . . . no, if it weren't for Alex's mother, none of this would have happened. Alex's beautifully dressed, wealthy mother, who was about as far along the spectrum from her mother as anyone could get. His mother made her mother look like . . . like what she had been—a woman struggling to raise three daughters alone after her husband had walked out and left her with nothing.

Alex's mother wouldn't know about things like that. Gretchen winced, remembering the expression of distaste on Mrs. Carson's face when she'd seen the French maid's costume. As if she'd just met a hooker or something. Gretchen took another bite of her hamburger. People like that didn't understand honest work. All they knew about was estates and trust funds.

Impatiently Gretchen took a sip of her coffee, which had cooled to lukewarm. A clock behind the counter slowly ticked off the minutes. Gretchen's irritation grew as she watched the hands creep along. One hour. That's what she had promised Alex. And one hour was all he was going to get. If he couldn't get rid of his mother in that length of time, he'd just have to face the consequences. It would serve him right. She wadded up her napkin, stuffed it into the Styrofoam cup and shoved the whole mess into an overflowing trash can. Then she gathered up her purse and the wet bag of sugar and walked out of the restaurant.

The misty rain had turned into a cold March downpour. Gretchen walked as fast as she could, tugging at her coat collar to stop the cold droplets from soaking the back of her neck. As she turned down the sidewalk to the apartment complex, she felt something hit her shoe. She took two more steps and it happened again. Too late she realized it was the sugar. She clutched the bag tighter to keep in from leaking, which split the wet paper and sent white granules cascading down her legs. The sugar caught in her net stockings, stuck to her wet legs and spilled into her shoes.

"Damn!" Gretchen exclaimed. She hurled the bag at the bushes and hurried along the sidewalk toward her apartment, ducking her head as sheets of rain stung her cheeks. The whole stupid mess was Alex's fault.

"You're soaked!" Alex exclaimed as she let herself into the apartment.

"Tell me about it," she retorted.

"And what's that stuff all over your feet?"

"Sugar."

"Sugar?"

"Yes, Yuppie, sugar!" Gretchen answered angrily. "If you hadn't given me that stupid sack of sugar, it wouldn't have gotten soaked with rain and split and spilled all over me."

Alex coughed to hide a grin. He wasn't sure what to do first. Gretchen was a mess, but a very appealing mess, even soaking wet and angry. Her cheeks were very pink and her lips almost red from the cold and very inviting. He watched a drop of water run across one softly arched eyebrow, drop down and catch in her thick lashes. What he wanted to do was not what he was going to do, he decided quickly.

"Listen, I'm sorry about what's happened," he apologized, taking her soggy coat from her shoulders. "I had no idea you'd get caught out in the rain. It's just that my mother..."

"*Your* mother. *Your* bicycle. *Your* aquarium..." Gretchen stopped abruptly as she spotted an oval object, covered with an old dish towel, on a stand next to the couch. "What is that thing?" Gretchen demanded, pointing at it.

"Oh, that," Alex answered vaguely. "I promised to keep it for my mother while she's in Europe. She and my Aunt Amelia spend every spring in France."

"Alex!" Gretchen exploded. "I don't care a whit about your Aunt Amelia. I want to know what that thing is you've brought into my living room."

"I just explained that," Alex answered, trying to decide exactly how to tell Gretchen what he was going to have to tell her. "While my mother is in France . . ."

But Gretchen wasn't listening. She stalked across the room and yanked off the cover, only to find herself staring through tiny white bars at the stupidest-looking bird she'd ever seen. It was bright yellow except for its head, which had a fringe of black feathers that looked like a misplaced dust ruffle.

"That is Tweety," Alex said tersely. "He's my mother's canary."

"Oh, no," Gretchen began, the pitch of her voice rising fast. "No birds. Fish are bad enough but no birds. I don't care how broke I am. I absolutely refuse to live with a stupid canary whose owner is in Europe."

Right on cue the canary chirped twice, as though tuning up, and then began trilling up and down the scale.

"Alex Carson, you get that thing out of here," Gretchen ordered. The canary sang louder. "You get it out of here tonight," she shouted. The louder she talked, the louder the bird sang.

Alex worked hard not to laugh. "Why don't we put the cover back on and you go take a bath," he suggested. "I can't possibly do anything with Tweety tonight."

"Well, you'd better figure something out by morning, Yuppie. Otherwise that bird goes, and you go with him," she threatened.

As soon as Alex dropped the cage cover back in place, the singing stopped. "Listen, Gretchen, I'm not exactly crazy about Tweety, either, but . . ."

"No buts and no more discussion. The bird goes tomorrow." Gretchen bent down and pulled off her wet shoes. "I'm going to take a bath," she said icily and disappeared into the bathroom, slamming the door behind her.

Alex paced up and down the hall outside the bathroom door for several minutes, feeling guilty. He'd given Gretchen a raw deal, and then he hadn't even been sympathetic. Seeing her standing there, soaking wet and covered with sugar, had been a hell of a lot funnier than if the situation had been reversed.

"Gretchen," he called through the closed door after the water stopped running.

No reply. She had every right to be mad. If she'd moved into his apartment and then told him to pretend he didn't live there because her mother was visiting, he'd have been mad, too. More than mad. Really steamed.

"Gretchen!" he called louder.

Several seconds passed, punctuated by some splashing. "I'm taking a bath," her muffled voice answered.

"I know you're taking a bath." He was shouting now. "I want to apologize."

"You what?"

"I want to apologize."

Gretchen slid deeper into the bubbles. He had to be kidding. "Forget it, Yuppie," she shouted back.

"No, I'm really sorry."

She thought he said he was sorry but she couldn't be sure. "I still can't hear you. I told you, I'm taking a bath."

"What did you say? I can't hear you."

This was one of the dumbest conversations she'd ever had. She didn't want to talk to him anyway.

"Gretchen, I can't hear you. Are you all right?"

"Damn!" Gretchen muttered, dropping the soap with an enormous splash.

Then she heard the door open. How dare he come into the bathroom! She jerked the shower curtain across the front of the tub. "Alex Carson, you get out of here right now!" she ordered.

"I'm not in there," he answered, his voice clear and easily understandable now that the door was open. "I was worried about you when you didn't answer me so I opened the door to make sure you're all right."

"Well, you can close it. I've been taking baths all by myself for twenty-five years and I haven't drowned once." She waited, but the door didn't close.

"Out, Yuppie!" she exclaimed, peeking around the curtain.

He was standing in the doorway surrounded by steam with that grin on his face that drove her wild.

"Actually, you're perfectly well covered behind that curtain," he observed, stepping inside. "You shouldn't mind if I come in. It's too hard to carry on a conversation through the door."

Gretchen snapped the shower curtain shut again and picked up her washcloth. "Who said we were going to carry on a conversation?"

"I did."

His voice was annoyingly calm.

"I really am sorry about everything that happened tonight," he continued, closing the toilet lid and sitting down. "But you said you had to work."

Gretchen stopped washing. "What do you mean I said I had to work?"

"You left me a note on the mirror saying you had to work tonight, and so I assumed you wouldn't be home."

"You mean that was why you asked if I'd be home tonight? Because your mother was coming and you didn't want her to know about me?"

The tone of Gretchen's voice had changed. A new emotion had crept in, one that might be loosely defined as rage. Alex tried to figure out what he'd done. He'd tried to plan everything so carefully. Bringing his mother to the apartment hadn't been absolutely necessary, but with the canary to deal with, it had been much easier. And he had made sure Gretchen wouldn't be home. He tried to remember exactly what his note had said, something about whether she'd be home. What was her answer? Something about being sorry but she had to work—that had struck him as rather odd when he read it, but he hadn't given it much thought at the time...

"Why did you think I wanted to know if you were going to be home?" Alex asked.

"It doesn't make any difference."

She sounded sullen and angry. He listened to the splashing behind the curtain and tried to imagine what part she was washing. Maybe her feet? Maybe not. He shifted uncomfortably. This conversation would be easier if he could see her, but not in her current state, not if he was going to concentrate on what she was saying.

"Gretchen, answer me," he demanded after several moments of silence. "Did you think I wanted you to go out with me? Is that why you thought I left the note?"

The splashing continued. "I told you, Yuppie, it doesn't make any difference."

At least that answered his question. No wonder she was mad. She'd thought he was asking her for a date, and then she'd come home to find out all he wanted was to get rid of her. "Gretchen, I'm really sorry. I would like to go out with you."

"Well, I wouldn't like to go out with you, so it doesn't make any difference anyway. Besides, I'm working every night."

"Not forever. You must have *some* free time."

"Nope."

"Then take some time off."

"I need the money."

"Why? To help your sister?"

"Never mind. I just need it."

Her elbow poked into the shower curtain, and Alex could see from her shadow that she was washing her back. "Would you like me to help you wash your back?" he offered.

"How do you know what I'm doing?" Gretchen demanded.

"Because I'm psychic. Do you want some help?"

"No."

"You're sure?"

She hesitated. Somehow she'd gotten sugar down inside her costume, and even after lying in the tub she felt as if it was still there. It would be very nice to have someone wash her back with the sweet-smelling soap, gently rubbing the washcloth back and forth. She remembered the sensation of the oil-soaked washcloth sliding across her face. That had felt so good. Maybe too good. She couldn't let him wash her back. "No, I'll do it." She knew she didn't sound very convincing.

A hand appeared around the edge of the curtain just in front of her.

"But Alex—"

"Hand me the washcloth. And the soap. I won't look."

6

HER BACK WAS WHITE and smooth, the skin wet with little streams of water running down. Alex knelt beside the tub. How could a flat expanse of bare flesh, totally plain and unmarked, be so incredibly arousing?

"I thought you were going to wash my back, Yuppie." Gretchen held her arms crossed over her breasts and rested her head on her bent knees. She didn't look around at him.

"I was getting the soap wet," Alex retorted. "And if you want your back washed, don't call me Yuppie." His hand trembled as he clutched the fat pink bar of soap and he raised up on his knees until he could press his body against the side of the tub.

"It must be wet by now," Gretchen said.

Alex didn't answer. Taking a deep breath, he started with her shoulders. The soap left tiny bubbles in its wake as he slid it across her skin, around and around in circular motions.

"Mmm," Gretchen said. "That feels good."

The soap moved faster, sliding downward, as though it had a life of its own. Alex squeezed the bar tighter and tighter, trying to maintain control, as he crisscrossed through the bubbles until the soap slipped out of his grasp and disappeared beneath the surface of the water.

"What happened?" Gretchen asked. She started to sit up but as she remembered her vulnerable position she bent forward again.

"I dropped the soap, but I think I see it." He pulled up his sweater sleeve and reached under the water. Just as he thought he had it, the soap glided away and his fingers encountered the soft curve of Gretchen's hip instead. He was leaning around her, his lips nearly against her skin, his lower body pressed tight against the side of the bathtub.

"No, here it is," Gretchen said. As she reached forward to grab the soap she had to uncover herself again.

Alex leaned back where he could see better. He'd said he wouldn't look, but that didn't matter now. He couldn't not look at her. Her breast curved perfectly toward its erect pink tip. He caught his lower lip between his teeth.

"Damn, I missed it." Giving up on the soap, Gretchen quickly covered her chest again.

Alex licked his lips. "Maybe we don't need the soap. We probably have enough already." With his wet hand, he touched her back, which was like silk. His fingers traced the path where the soap bar had been, gliding just as easily across her skin. Again he started with her shoulders, his whole body swaying almost imperceptibly with the rhythm of his hand.

Gretchen didn't move. She didn't know what she'd been thinking when she agreed to let him wash her back, but she knew exactly what she was thinking now. His hand kept working in ever broadening circles. She had trouble sitting still. He was moving toward her left side, where she sometimes was ticklish, but not tonight. Tonight the sensation was one of liquid heat flowing inward to a central point. The bathwater was tepid, but Gretchen wouldn't have been at all surprised to see steam rising from the surface where she touched it. She should tell Alex to stop. Actually, she was going to tell him to stop. In just a few moments.

"I guess I'd better start washing the soap off," he said, his voice husky.

"That's a good idea," she heard herself agree.

She felt handfuls of water pouring across her back. His movements were random, producing intermittent tingling sensations both where he touched her and where he didn't. *He's almost through. He'll stop on his own now,* she thought, *and I won't have to say anything.*

Alex pulled up his other sweater sleeve and cupped water in both hands, following its flow down her back with his fingers. He heard her gasp. Her head was still buried against her knees and she was holding her arms loosely against herself so that the curve of her breasts was clearly visible. His hands moved in tandem around her to seek the softness of those curves. Her breasts were just as he'd imagined, softer by far than her back, the skin even smoother if that were possible.

Gretchen tensed but didn't pull away. "That's not my back, Yuppie," she said in a muffled voice.

"I know." His hands continued their exploration, moving around her.

Gretchen was on fire. The heat that had built to intense proportions spread wildly through her and she sat up, all pretense of modesty forgotten. Her breath came in short pants. He was still touching her, his fingers insistent until she turned toward him and his mouth took their place.

She arched her neck, tilting her head backward as she drank in the persistent pleasure.

"Alex—"

His mouth moved upward. "You are absolutely delicious," he murmured as his lips nibbled her skin. Wet skin touched him, slippery and yielding.

Gretchen's fantasies ran free. She imagined he was naked against her, sinking into warm water that swirled around their bodies. She reached up and stroked the back of his neck. "I'm getting you wet," she told him.

"I know." His hands searched the curve of her hips, moving beneath the thin bubbles that floated across her lap.

Her body trembled, and the fantasy swirled around her again. They were sinking deeper into the water and it was growing hotter and her thighs were pressing hard together against a heat that was driving upward. They were circling in a whirlpool. She was going to be swept under the water. She could feel it coming. Then her arms scraped against the coarse wool of his sweater, and she opened her eyes.

Alex was watching her, his lips open, his eyes smoldering. She saw him like a freeze frame in a movie; Alex Carson, the rich yuppie who was sharing her apartment, the man she'd have to face in the morning, and the next morning, and maybe for weeks to come. She closed her eyes again, but the fantasy didn't come back.

Alex's hand stopped moving. "Gretchen, what's the matter?"

"Nothing," she whispered, leaning up to press her cheek against his.

"Don't lie to me. What happened?"

"I don't know."

He clasped her cheeks between dripping hands and held her away from him, forcing her to look at him. They'd been together, swept along by an enormous force that just kept building and building until suddenly she'd veered off and he'd been alone. "You don't want this?" His whole body was shaking and his voice was harsh.

"Yes, Alex, I did—"

He dropped his hands and sat back against his feet. "But you don't now."

Gretchen was near tears. "I don't know what happened. All of a sudden I thought about the future and about sharing the apartment with you and how we have to go on—"

"Dammit, Gretchen, if you were going to back out you could have done it sooner."

He was right. She knew he was right. She never should have let him into the bathroom, never should have agreed to have him wash her back. "Wait a minute, Yuppie!" She scooped up the soggy washcloth and held it firmly in front of her. "I didn't invite you into the bathroom. You barged in all by yourself. And I wasn't the one who wanted *you* to wash *my* back. I didn't even agree to it."

Alex stood up and strode across the bathroom. His body was behind the partially closed door when he turned to face her. "You damn well didn't fight it very hard. Next time—"

"There won't be a next time," Gretchen interrupted.

"Damn right there won't." He slammed the door.

"And make sure you get rid of that stupid canary," she shouted after him. He didn't answer. Gretchen shivered. The bathwater had turned to ice, and she was suddenly very cold. She fished the slimy soap out of the tub and laid it in the dish, then rubbed her hand across the washcloth. All she wanted was to be dry and warm and in bed—by herself—where she could go to sleep and forget the day had ever happened.

ALEX WAS STILL OUT OF SORTS the next day. He didn't know whether the problem was Gretchen or the canary. All he knew was that it was hard to be inconspicuous on a busy street when you were carrying a bird cage. At least the cover kept the stupid bird quiet. Alex pushed open the office door and was standing in the middle of the reception room trying to decide where to put the cage when he heard his dental partner's voice behind him.

"So how's your sex life?"

Alex swung around so hard he almost dropped Tweety. His partner was leaning against the reception desk studying the appointment book.

"What sex life?" Alex growled.

"Could it be I've touched a sore spot?" Ed chuckled, not looking up.

"You could put it that way." Alex shoved a stack of magazines to one end of a table in the reception room and set down the bird cage. "I've had a lousy weekend."

"Haven't managed to get the blond bombshell in the sack yet, huh?"

"No, I haven't," Alex exploded. "And I don't want to discuss it, either."

Ed chuckled again. "That's rather obvious. Well, give her another try. Maybe your disposition will improve if you have an outlet for your frustration."

Ignoring Ed, Alex unpinned the towel that covered Tweety's cage. With the sudden influx of light, Tweety blinked twice and hopped up on his swinging perch. He let out two tentative peeps.

"What the hell is that?" Ed demanded, striding across the office for a closer look.

"My mother's canary."

Tweety cocked his head, trilled half an octave, then swung back and forth.

"Why do you have your mother's canary? Or shouldn't I ask?"

"I'm baby-sitting while she's in Europe." Alex pulled off his jacket and hung it on the coatrack. Without his bike helmet, it seemed as if something was missing. He hated driving to work, but he couldn't transport a canary and ride his bike at the same time.

Ed walked all the way around the cage, staring at the bird, which had hopped over to his feeder and was happily scattering seed in every direction. Then Ed looked directly at Alex. "More to the point, why do you have your mother's canary spraying birdseed all over our reception room?"

Alex sighed. Obviously Ed wasn't big on canaries, either. "I'd planned to keep him at the apartment, but Gretchen refused."

"And that was what started your problems with her, right?"

"Something like that."

Ed nodded knowingly. "And things went from bad to worse and when it was all over, you wanted to and she didn't and it had nothing to do with the canary."

Alex shoved some of the scattered birdseed under the table with his foot. "Since when are you so damned perceptive?"

"Hardly an original scenario," Ed observed. "You ought to be glad you aren't thirty years older. In my day it was fashionable for the male to go for it and the female to refuse. Damned frustrating."

"Things haven't changed," Alex noted sourly. He pulled on his light blue clinic jacket. "It's still damned frustrating."

"Oh, yeah? From what I read, women nowadays are ready to go to it anywhere, any time." He paced to the other side of the receptionist desk and opened the appointment book again.

Alex pictured Gretchen in the bathtub. He understood how Ed might think that. Actually, he'd thought so, too.

"Must depend on the woman," Ed continued. He held his glasses up to the light, shook his head and began cleaning them. "Some women probably still need some wining and dining, you know, the proper buildup."

"I don't see what dinner has to do with sex," Alex answered.

"Did you ever see *Tom Jones*?" Ed inquired. "In that movie, dinner was sex, or at least a pretty fair reenactment." He checked the glasses and began cleaning again. "But that's not what I meant. For some women, going to dinner and getting flowers is part of the foreplay. It seems to warm them up."

Alex frowned. He thought about the note he'd left for Gretchen, and her voice echoed in his memory. "Is that why you wanted to know if I had plans? Because your mother was coming?" Hardly something that would warm someone up. He had come on pretty strong, but she was so damned sexy. And there was no doubt in his mind that she'd wanted it, too, just like he had. He did have to admit he'd never had an actual date with her. The closest he'd come was that rainy day when they ate Chinese take-out. But that was hardly a date. Maybe he'd been a little hasty.

"This woman doesn't have time to go to dinner," he told Ed. "All she does is work."

"What did you say she does again?"

"Works for an outfit called Shenanigans. She pops out of cakes at bachelor parties, wears sexy costumes to deliver helium balloons, stuff like that. She's supposed to be a teacher but she lost her job."

"She chose an interesting replacement," Ed noted. "You like her?"

Alex shrugged. "I guess so." He hadn't really thought about it in those terms. At the beginning he'd thought

Gretchen was an airhead, but now that he was getting to know her, he'd changed his mind. "Yeah, I guess I do like her," he added, half to himself. Actually, he realized he liked her a lot. That was part of the problem. Somewhere along the line he'd started to care how she felt and what she thought. That had been the point when sex for the sake of sex had lost its appeal. He wanted more from Gretchen now, and for some reason things weren't working out.

Ed interrupted his thoughts. "So why don't you take her out?"

"I told you, she works all the time."

"So, show some ingenuity. Pick her up after work and have a late dinner somewhere. A little candlelight, soft music."

"I can't do that," Alex protested. "She doesn't get through till midnight, and I get up at six o'clock."

Ed leaned on his elbows and stared at Alex across the desk. "Me, I'm an old man. I need my beauty sleep. But you, you're young—what are you, thirty? And you're telling me you've got a shot at some sexy broad and you're going to blow it because you want to sleep?" He shook his head. Before Alex could answer, he disappeared into examining room three, at the rear of the office.

Alex scowled at his partner's disappearing form and then turned to the canary, which was singing exuberantly. "Damned bird," he muttered, kicking at the seed scattered on the carpet.

"He sure has a good, loud song," observed a voice near the office door.

Alex looked up to see John Halvorsen in the doorway leaning on his cane.

"I didn't mean to startle you," the old man said. "I saw you in here and thought I'd stop by before you got busy for the day. I want to give you the news on Susan. She says you sent her a clown with a red balloon."

Alex smiled. He'd felt bad about not getting over to see the little girl in person, but maybe asking Gretchen to give her the balloon had been even better. "How is she?" Alex asked. "Will she be coming home soon?"

Mr. Halvorsen shook his head. "They're going to run some more tests and then they say if she's strong enough she might need an operation."

Alex thought about the energetic little girl flying down the sidewalk on her roller skates. "What kind of operation?"

"I don't know exactly. They say there's something the matter with the blood vessels around her heart from having strep throat a few years back, but they seem to think they can fix it."

Probably some kind of a bypass or artery replacement, Alex thought. Susan seemed so little to have to go through an ordeal like that. "They can do a lot these days," Alex said encouragingly. "Tell her we're all thinking about her."

"I will," Mr. Halvorsen agreed, "and, Dr. Carson, do you think you could keep that clown coming? She's been there two or three times now, and Susan really likes her."

"No problem," Alex assured him. He knew Gretchen would keep going back even if he didn't ask her.

Mr. Halvorsen eyed the canary, which was still singing loudly. "That bird sure is a strange one. Too bad Susan can't see him."

"Too bad she can't *have* him," Alex said. He wondered if there was any way to persuade the hospital to adopt a resident canary on a temporary basis.

Once Mr. Halvorsen was gone, Alex checked the appointment book and went to prepare for his first patient. His conversation with Susan's grandfather bothered him all day, and he decided he'd visit the girl as soon as possible. Maybe he'd take Gretchen with him and they could play a game of Parcheesi. But after the past weekend he wasn't sure Gretchen would even speak to him, much less go with him to the hospital.

THE PHONE WAS RINGING when he unlocked the apartment door that evening. As he raced inside to catch it before the last ring, he tripped on his bike and nearly fell flat. "Damn!" he muttered, rubbing his shin and grabbing the phone at the same time. He hated to admit it, but he could understand why the bike might annoy Gretchen.

"I'm looking for Gretchen Bauer," the gravelly voice on the phone line said.

There was something about the voice Alex didn't like. "She's not here. Would you like to leave a message?" He opened the table drawer and dug unsuccessfully for a pencil.

"When's she coming home?"

Alex was tempted to say it was none of his business, but it was Gretchen's phone call. "I don't know. Is there a message?"

"Tell her Lew's looking for her."

The phone clicked and Alex hung up in disgust. Surely he wasn't a friend of Gretchen's. Maybe he'd been calling about a job. Whatever it was, Gretchen would be better off without it. A little more searching through the cluttered drawer produced a ballpoint pen and a scrap of paper. He scrawled a brief note about the phone call and left it on the table where Gretchen would find it. Then he headed for the kitchen to do something about his dinner. He was just adding some bean sprouts to his stir-fry chicken and vegetables when he heard the front door open.

"Gretchen?" When she appeared in the kitchen doorway, he broke into a grin. She was wearing the French maid outfit again tonight. She must have run it through the wash because there wasn't a grain of sugar anywhere. He grinned even more broadly at the memory of her, soaking wet, with sugar stuck all over. She was the only woman he knew who could be so appealing under such adverse circumstances. Damn, he really wanted to take her to bed. He was still smarting from her refusal the other night. And what irritated him almost as much was how glad he was to see her now. "What are you doing home so early?"

Gretchen dropped her coat over the back of a kitchen chair. "My five o'clock show was a mistake on the schedule. I don't actually have to do a performance until nine tonight." She didn't add that when she'd found out about the mistake she almost hadn't come home. She'd known Alex would be there and she didn't want to face him. She didn't know what to say. Stalling for time while she thought of the right words, she studied the design on the worn linoleum floor. She'd never really noticed the little blue flecks in the pattern before. Maybe if she scrubbed the floor more often she would have known what it looked like. Apprehensively she looked up. Alex was turned away from her, stirring something in his wok. "I'm sorry about the other night," she said in a small voice.

Alex started to chuckle.

"Don't you dare laugh at me. I'm trying to be nice and apologize—for something that I was not entirely responsible for, I might add—and you're making fun of me."

"I'm not making fun of you," Alex protested. "I'm just laughing at the whole situation. It's pretty funny when you think about it."

"There's nothing funny about it at all." But despite her words she felt the corners of her mouth twitching and a second later she was laughing with him. How could she be so angry with Alex and yet be laughing with him? This man was going to drive her out of her mind.

Alex dropped the chopsticks into his wok and took two steps toward her. Instinctively, Gretchen backed away.

"Oh, no, you don't. I can see that gleam in your eye, and that's what gets us into all this trouble."

Alex gazed openly at the fullness of her breasts above the bodice of her costume. "It's not the gleam in my eye that gets us into trouble. It's your cute, seductive shape." He reached out to take her in his arms.

Quickly Gretchen sidestepped him and grabbed her coat from the chair. "My shape's effect on you is an easy problem to solve." She pulled on her coat, buttoned it completely and sat down in the chair. "There will be absolutely no more of this nonsense. We're roommates. Nothing more. Understood, Yuppie?"

Wordlessly, Alex shrugged. Putting her coat on didn't make a damned bit of difference. Her huge blue eyes sparkled as she spoke, and her cheeks were flushed with color. Her soft blond hair—he had finally decided *flaxen* was the word to describe the color—curled softly around her face. Her lips were pursed, begging to be kissed.

Gretchen pulled her chair up to the table. "Well, I'm glad we've finally got all this cleared up." She wasn't at all sure they were straight about anything, but it seemed like a good idea to be firm and to take a positive approach. She didn't want to end up in another situation like the other night in the bathtub.

"Uh, right. It's good to be clear about these things. Right." Alex picked up his chopsticks and turned away. All he had to do was convince his body to listen to what he was saying, instead of what he was thinking.

Gretchen unbuttoned the top two buttons of her coat but left it on. She tucked a napkin in her lap. "Now, Yuppie, where's my dinner? I'm starving."

"Coming right up." Willing his body under control, Alex dumped the rest of the bean sprouts in the wok, stirred and reached for two plates. As he set Gretchen's meal on the table, her hair brushed lightly against his arm, and he inhaled sharply.

"Something the matter?" She looked up, trying to ignore the tingling in her body she felt every time he got near her.

"Nope, nothing's wrong." Nonchalantly, he swung into his chair across from her and took a bite of chicken.

"This is good stir-fry." Keep the situation casual, she told herself, and all the sensuous feelings will disappear. "You're not a bad cook, Yuppie."

Alex watched as she took a bite of bamboo shoot. "Thanks. The electric wok helps. I think I'm going to get a rice cooker, too."

Gretchen continued to eat hungrily, deliberately not looking at him. After her impassioned declaration, she wasn't about to give him any idea what he was doing to her. She wiped her damp palms on her napkin. "You know, I was thinking," she began. It was hard to talk with him so close. She wished the table were bigger.

"What's that?"

"Well, it's not even six o'clock, and I don't have to be at my next show until nine. That's almost three more hours we have to spend together. Maybe it would be a good idea if we thought of something to do—"

"I can think of plenty of things to do," Alex interjected. "We could start by taking off your coat."

"That's not what I mean," Gretchen replied firmly. Heat began curling and rising inside her. "I had in mind a game—"

"A game, that's a great idea." Alex grinned at her.

"Not that kind of game! I meant checkers, or gin rummy, or something like that." Why did he have to make this so damn difficult?

"Gin rummy. Yeah, gin rummy." Alex didn't want to play gin rummy any more than he wanted to play checkers. And he could tell gin rummy wasn't the foremost thing on her mind, either. But if she wanted to ignore what was going on, he sure wasn't going to press the issue. Not after the other night in the bathroom.

"All right," he agreed. "We'll play gin." No, Alex thought as soon as he'd said it, they wouldn't play gin. If she was so into chastity suddenly, he'd do her one better. He'd even provide a chaperon. "I've got another idea," he said. "I've got a Parcheesi game in the closet. We can go to the hospital and play Parcheesi with Susan."

"You want to go to the hospital tonight?" Gretchen put down her fork, no longer interested in the last few bites of her dinner.

"Why not?" Alex questioned. "Susan's grandfather stopped by the office today and said she's still having tests and she's getting lonesome and bored." He winked at Gretchen. "Besides, she'd keep us out of trouble." He stood up and took their two dinner plates to the sink.

Gretchen sat quietly, watching Alex. What he said made perfect sense, except that she wasn't going to do it.

"I think I'll pass," she said, wadding up her napkin. "You go ahead."

Alex frowned. He'd thought she'd like the idea. "Parcheesi isn't any fun with two," he replied.

"You can always play checkers." Gretchen stood up, unbuttoning her coat but holding it closed. "Maybe I'll take a quick shower and a nap before I go back to work."

Alex lifted both plates out of the soapy water, rinsed them and put them in the drainer. Everything had been fine until he'd suggested the hospital. Then he'd hit a wall. She obviously didn't want to visit Susan—or she was afraid to. He turned and met her eyes but she quickly looked away. So he wasn't imagining things. "What's with you, Gretchen?" he asked bluntly.

"I don't know what you mean," she retorted. "I go to the hospital every Saturday. Why is it such a big deal if I pass on it tonight?"

True, Alex thought, she did go every Saturday, but with one difference. He was beginning to understand the problem. "Clara the Clown goes to the hospital on Saturdays, Gretchen," Alex said softly.

Gretchen paced into the living room and Alex followed her. She hadn't expected him to have so much insight. She'd known for a long time that the clown costume was a crutch. She wasn't prepared for anyone else to know, especially Alex. "You probably think I'm really weak, don't you?" she asked defensively.

"Nope," Alex answered. "I just think you need to cut loose from your past. Your sister has been dead for twelve years and yet you're still reliving it."

Gretchen spun around. "That's not true!"

"Isn't it?" Alex hoped he hadn't made a mistake by confronting her, but he held his ground. If they ever were going to work out this crazy relationship growing up between them, they had to be honest with each other. And honest with themselves.

Flinging her coat over a chair, Gretchen sat down on the couch and stared into space. "When Nancy died, it was awful for all of us," she said in a flat voice. "Joyce and I always thought there must have been something we could have done to prevent it. As an adult I know that isn't true, but . . ."

"But you still feel guilty?" He sat beside her and took her hand.

"Silly, isn't it?" She tried to smile.

"No, not silly," he said, feeling a deep compassion for her. "Just one of those ghosts hanging around from something that never quite got settled inside you. We all have them." He stroked her hand gently and suddenly felt very protective. "I'm sorry I even brought up going to the hospital. It was a lousy idea."

Gretchen hesitated. Even while forcing herself to go through all those hospital visits as Clara, she'd never seen the problem quite so clearly as she did at that moment. And as much as she wanted to reject it, she also saw a solution. "I'm not sure going to see Susan is such a bad idea," she said in a barely audible voice.

"But you just said—"

"I know what I just said, Yuppie."

Her big blue eyes were fired with that determination he often saw there.

"But haven't you ever heard of a woman changing her mind?"

Alex grinned. He wasn't about to argue that. "Should I point out that you're still disguised as a French maid?" he asked her.

Gretchen looked down at her outfit and managed a shaky laugh. "Not too appropriate, huh?" She disappeared into her bedroom to change into slacks and a sweater.

ON THE WAY TO THE HOSPITAL Gretchen talked to Alex about Parcheesi, which she hadn't played in years. The conversation turned from that to the weather and then to her busy schedule. Underlying the casual banter, she felt a sense of foreboding mixed with an unexpected anticipation. She didn't want to go. But, at the same time, she wanted to have done it.

When they entered the hospital lobby, Gretchen's step slowed. As Clara, she was always the center of attention. She and everyone else were focused on the clown. Now she saw the hospital itself and the people, some of them laughing and talking, others silent and worried, on their way to visit friends and loved ones. She was one of them again.

That was the moment when she might have backed out if Alex hadn't taken her hand. She squeezed tight, telling him all the things she couldn't say, and he smiled down at her.

"Just keep remembering it's Susan we're going to visit," he told her as they got on the elevator.

"I'm trying," she whispered back. "Believe me, I'm trying." She didn't let go of his hand.

The door to 4-B was open and from the hallway Gretchen could see Susan sitting in bed talking to her teddy bear. For a moment she froze, chilled by a sudden blizzard of memories that swept over her. Then she felt Alex's arm slip around her. Slowly, the child sitting there in the bed became Susan Halvorsen, a little girl who needed some company to get through a long, boring day.

"Hi there, Suzy Q," Gretchen called out as she walked briskly into the room.

"Clara," came Susan's delighted squeal from the bed, followed by a puzzled expression. "You're not Clara! But that's what she calls me."

Alex laughed and took Gretchen's hand. "This is my friend Gretchen," he said. "She's also a friend of Clara's."

"But why do you call me Susie Q?"

Gretchen laughed and walked over to the side of the bed. "Because you look like a Susie Q," she answered.

Susan looked her over carefully. "Do you play games?"

Gretchen nodded solemnly. "I am a very good game player."

"Then I'm going to like you," Susan announced, "because you're a lot like Clara."

"She even plays Parcheesi," Alex added, holding up the game so that Susan could see it. For just an instant he met Gretchen's eyes across the bed and he knew everything was all right. She was relaxed and happy and probably very much the first-grade teacher he had not ever seen before.

For the next hour Alex and Gretchen and Susan gathered around the Parcheesi board, talking and laughing as much as they played. Finally they abandoned the game altogether, and Gretchen spent a considerable amount of time braiding Susan's hair. Just before they left, she tied a ribbon around the neck of Susan's teddy bear, with a promise to bring more ribbons the next time she visited.

"Maybe you could send them with Clara on Saturday," Susan suggested.

From her expression, Gretchen couldn't be sure whether she knew or not. "I'll try to arrange it," she promised.

"See you," Susan said with a wave.

"See you," Alex and Gretchen answered in unison.

Alex could feel the spring in Gretchen's step as she walked down the hall with his arm around her. "Are you glad you came?" he asked while they waited for the elevator.

When she looked up at him, her smile said it all. "Thanks, Alex," she answered softly. "I couldn't have done it without you." She hesitated for a long moment. "I sure hope Susan's going to be all right," she added.

"But it's not tearing you apart the same way as before?"

Gretchen shook her head. "I just want it for her very, very much."

"Me, too," Alex agreed. "She's a neat little kid." The elevator doors opened before he could give Gretchen a hug.

As they drove to the apartment Alex found himself wishing Gretchen didn't have a performance that evening. He'd like to spend more time with her, maybe stop for a cup of coffee at the deli or something. He realized he really didn't know very much about her. He wondered what kind of little girl she had been. A handful, he suspected. Probably took dancing lessons, maybe drama in high school, which had eventually led to her job with Shenanigans. None of it was really too important, but for some reason he just wanted to know. He reached across the gearshift in his Porsche and took Gretchen's hand.

Echoing his thoughts, she said, "I wish I didn't have to go to work tonight . . ." Her voice trailed off.

"Maybe, on your next free evening, we could go to a movie, or out to dinner, or something." Damn! He sounded like a high-school kid asking for his first date.

Gretchen looked over at him and smiled. "All right, maybe a movie, or dinner, or something, would be kind of nice."

Alex pulled his car alongside her pink Volkswagen and watched while she gathered up her purse, gloves and costume bag. As she started to open the door he took her arm and stopped her from getting out. "I'll leave you a note on the mirror, if that's all right."

Gretchen nodded. "A note on the mirror is fine." Then she paused for a minute before she leaned over and kissed him lightly on the lips. "See you later, Yuppie." She grinned and climbed out of the Porsche.

Alex watched Gretchen's car all the way down Wilson Boulevard until the taillights blurred with all the other lights along the street. He could still taste her lips, warm and sweet, and he wanted to hold her, not take her to bed, at least not right then, just hold her. He parked his Porsche and glanced up at the dark apartment. Damn, he didn't want to go in there alone. Why the hell did she have to work every single night? He was used to spending lots of time with the women he dated. Of course he wasn't actually dating Gretchen, he realized, walking up the stairs toward the apartment. Ironically, in his case he was living with her.

In the apartment, he flipped on the television and tried to interest himself in a sitcom, but after a few minutes he turned it off and wandered into the kitchen to get a snack. Gretchen's schedule was tacked on a bulletin board next to the refrigerator. Two parties were listed for tonight, the one that had been canceled and another one with a star beside it, whatever that meant. She wouldn't be home any time soon.

He went into the living room and picked up a news-magazine that had come the day before. He wasn't interested in it, either. Maybe he would meet Gretchen after work. Then he remembered she had her car with her. That didn't matter, he decided. They could just go somewhere nearby for something to eat and pick up her car on the way home. He checked his watch. If he hurried, he could watch her perform.

The evening suddenly looked more promising. He hurried downstairs. As he pulled his Porsche out onto the street and checked the rearview mirror, he noted a black Corvette pulling out from a parking space about a half a block behind him. Flashy car, but impractical, he thought as he turned the corner. Several blocks later, he checked the mirror again and the Corvette was still behind him. After that he didn't notice because the traffic got heavy and he was concentrating on finding the hotel where Gretchen was working. He wanted to be sure to get there in time to catch her act.

7

GRETCHEN CURLED HER BODY into a ball as the cardboard replica of a wedding cake was lowered slowly over her. People had no idea how hot it was inside a cardboard cake. And dark. And cramped. As small as she was, she barely fit. Her bridal costume might be gorgeous, but it was also tight, and the veil itched when it rubbed her bare shoulders.

Of course, from the outside everything looked lovely. The magnificent three-tier cake was centered on a table covered with immaculate linen. Tapered white candles on each side were set in small bouquets of fresh flowers. The whole scene appeared authentic, even to the tiny beribboned figures of a bride and groom, which adorned the thin tissue-paper covering on the top of the cake.

That didn't change the fact that Gretchen was tired and hot and she wanted to go home to bed. But it wouldn't be much longer now before the rolling table with the cake would be moved into a prominent position in the ballroom. She'd take over from there.

Through the thin frosted walls of the cake Gretchen could hear band music from the hotel ballroom, punctuated by raucous laughter. It sounded as if the bachelor party was in full swing. As she wiggled her toes and hugged her knees tighter, Gretchen heard a familiar voice. The sound was faint at first, then louder, as though the man were coming into the room. She pressed her ear against the wall of the cake and listened carefully but didn't hear anything more.

Shifting her weight sideways, she tried to see out through a small slit in the cardboard. After a moment, she caught the slightest glimpse of a man's face, its muscles twitching under rough, pallid skin. Her stomach lurched. Then she saw the bald head and the stub of a cigar in his mouth and she was sure. It was Lew from the pawnshop. How could he know she was there?

Then the voice faded and Gretchen held her breath. All she could hear was the distant music and the beating of her own heart. Lew was no longer in sight. Clammy perspiration gathered on her neck. Could he be there by coincidence? She doubted it. More likely he was looking for her.

Before she had time to dwell on the possibility, she felt the table moving and heard the pop-rock beat of the "Wedding March" throbbing loudly. She patted the wedding veil in place over her blond curls and adjusted a shoulder strap on the bridal costume. As the table lurched to a stop, a drumroll reverberated through the ballroom. Gretchen tensed, forcing herself to concentrate.

The cymbals crashed, and on the upbeat she burst through the top of the wedding cake into the spotlight. The crowd went wild. With big blue eyes she surveyed the room full of cheering, applauding men, while the lights played across the dazzling white sequins of her costume. After giving the audience a glowing smile, she stepped gracefully out of the cake and entwined herself around the startled groom. A new round of cheers and male laughter filled the hot, smoky room.

As the men clustered around them, the groom muttered an embarrassed expletive. Gretchen peered anxiously over his shoulder at the assembled group, searching for any sign of Lew. She spotted him in the far corner near the door, chewing his cigar and watching her. Gretchen realized immediately she was going to have to find another way out, and she was going to have to do it fast.

A waiter, carrying a tray of canapés, hurried past them. He must have come from somewhere. She looked behind him just in time to see the door to the kitchen swing shut and realized she could ease out through the back while the men screened her from Lew's weasel eyes. Dispensing with the normal goodbyes, she pulled away from the groom and took off past the buffet table. She'd covered about half the distance to the kitchen when a pair of hands grabbed her shoulders from behind.

"How dare you!" She spun around. But, instead of Lew from the pawnshop, the man holding her was Alex Carson. Gretchen's eyes widened. She stopped trying to pull away. "Alex," she said, almost in a whisper. "What are you doing here?"

"You were absolutely magnificent." He broke into a grin and relaxed his grip on her shoulders. "When you said you popped out of cakes, I had no idea you did it like that."

"Thank you, but how did you find me? And why? Is something the matter?"

"Not a thing. I thought you might like to go get something to eat after you finished work."

Gretchen was more confused than before. She had been expecting him to take her out. She just hadn't thought it would happen so soon or quite this way. "But, Alex, it's so late, nearly midnight."

Alex grinned. "This seems to be the only time that both you and I are free when one of us isn't sleeping. If you don't want to go out, that's all right," he told her. "I just thought it might be fun."

Gretchen's whole face lit up with a delighted smile. "Hey, Yuppie, once in a while you manage to come up with a great idea. It won't take me a minute to change and get my coat." She turned and started toward the ladies' room. Before she had taken two steps, she found herself looking directly into Lew's small, protruding eyes.

"You're late," he announced without prelude.

Gretchen stepped backward and pressed securely against Alex. "I'm not! I left a note explaining."

"You don't leave notes, lady. You leave cash. That's the deal."

"But I couldn't." Gretchen's heart was pounding.

"You must have done all right tonight," Lew observed. His outstretched palm, with yellowed, stubby fingers, extended toward her. "Hand it over."

"I haven't been paid yet." Gretchen felt Alex's hands at her waist moving her aside, and then he was towering over Lew.

"What seems to be the problem?" Alex demanded. Gretchen had never heard his voice sound like that.

"Your girlfriend thinks she can get away with holding out on me," Lew answered. "She better ante up."

"I don't know what your problem is, buddy, but it's time for you to take off." Alex took a menacing step toward Lew, but the smaller man didn't back down.

"Wrong." Lew's eyes narrowed. "Your girlfriend's the one with the problem. She either pays up or she's in big trouble." He turned on his heel and disappeared into the crowd.

Gretchen looked at Alex's clenched fists and put a restraining hand on his arm. "Let's just go home, Alex."

Alex didn't move. Slowly he turned toward Gretchen. "What the hell is going on?"

"It doesn't matter," she answered. "I just want to go home." She darted through the crowd of men and out the door of the ballroom with Alex close behind her. By the time she'd retrieved her coat and gone outside to get into her car, he was nowhere in sight. But when she pulled the Volkswagen out of its parking space, Alex's Porsche pulled out right behind her. He followed her closely all the way home, and as she turned her key in the apartment door, she heard his footsteps on the stairs.

"Now you're going to tell me what the hell is going on," he commanded once they were inside the apartment.

Gretchen threw her coat down on the chair and faced him, her mouth set and her eyes flashing. "And if I don't?"

Alex didn't waver. "You're going to. Why does that guy think you owe him money?"

"Because I do," Gretchen blurted out.

From his startled expression, Alex obviously had expected some other answer. "For what?"

"To repay a loan," Gretchen said in a steady voice. "Does that satisfy you?"

Alex didn't try to hide his exasperation. "You borrowed money from *him*?"

"Yes, I did." Gretchen's voice rose. "And I hated it, but I didn't have any choice. You wouldn't understand something like that. You don't know what it means—"

Alex cut her off. "The bastard's nothing but a loan shark! What did you think you were doing?"

"I knew exactly what I was doing," Gretchen shouted at him. "I was keeping Joyce in medical school, and it worked, and I'm not sorry."

"You damned well could have figured out some better way to do it."

"All right, Yuppie, just exactly what would you suggest I do? I don't have a portfolio of stocks and bonds or an expensive car or a Swiss bank account to draw on just in case I should need a little something extra."

Alex crammed his hands into his pants pockets and glared at her. "Come off it, Gretchen. Neither do I, and you know it." He paced to the kitchen then to the living room where he sat on the couch, stretching his legs in front of him. "If you'd quit taking potshots at me, maybe we could figure something out. Why don't you come sit down?"

"Because I don't feel like sitting down. It's one o'clock in the morning. I feel like going to bed." She kicked off her shoes and padded across the room to stand by the radiator where she'd be warmer.

"How much did you borrow from this guy?" Alex asked.

"Five thousand dollars."

"On what terms?"

Gretchen hesitated. The whole thing was none of his business. He was probably going to make fun of her and make her feel like some incompetent idiot if she told him. But she really needed to talk to someone. Surely Lew wouldn't hurt her, not physically hurt her, but he could make her life pretty miserable. And inside, that tiny element of doubt about what actually might happen if she couldn't pay on time kept nagging at her. As much as she hated to admit it, she was scared.

"The terms, Gretchen," Alex repeated. "What were the terms of the loan?"

"I have to pay him three hundred dollars every Wednesday."

"For how long?"

"Six months...actually now it's six months and a week because I skipped the last payment."

"Damn," Alex muttered. He closed his eyes for a moment. "Do you know what that interest rate it?"

"No, and I don't want to know," Gretchen retorted. "All I know is I can probably swing the three hundred dollars a week most of the time, except last week I had to get my car fixed. I explained that to him—"

"You don't explain to people like that, Gretchen. Dammit! Did you ever consider borrowing the money from a bank?"

"Don't you lecture me, Alex Carson! You don't have any idea what it's like to be broke. I promised Joyce. She worked to send me to school—now I'm helping her." Gretchen threw up her hands in disgust. She could talk all night and never make him understand. "Never mind. I knew you wouldn't be any help." She stalked across the room.

"Gretchen, wait." Alex was on his feet. "We've got to solve this. That guy won't leave you alone until he gets his money."

Halfway to her bedroom, Gretchen turned around. "I've been solving my problems all my life and I'll solve this one, too. I don't need any help from a ...a... *yuppie!*"

She slammed the bedroom door as hard as she could and then locked it with a loud snap. Once she was alone, she collapsed in a heap on the bed and curled up around her pillow. This time she'd really made a mess. And she didn't need Alex Carson or anyone else to point it out to her. He was cold and heartless and uncaring...and he was right. She shouldn't have borrowed the money from Lew. But she really hadn't had any choice. That was the part Alex couldn't comprehend. She wished she could talk to him but even trying was pointless. He'd reacted exactly the way she'd expected. And of course he would. When it came to money, the world was composed of haves and have nots.

Neither understood the other and that was just the way it was.

Gretchen sat up and set her jaw determinedly. All her life she'd solved her problems herself and this time was no exception. She'd simply have to come up with the money somehow. Maybe in the morning something would occur to her, or maybe Trudy would have an idea. Something would work out. It always did.

When she woke up the next day, the clock read noon and she was still exhausted. The apartment was silent, which meant Alex was gone. She wondered how much sleep he'd had. If he was tired all day, it served him right for butting into her affairs, she decided, as she walked sleepily toward the bathroom, which still smelled vaguely of aftershave. Alex's toothbrush protruded from a cup on the vanity, next to his Water Pik. His sweatshirt was hanging on the hook on the back of the door. And his underwear was all over the shower, she discovered as she was about to step in.

"Alex Carson, you are the most obnoxious roommate!" she exclaimed. She pulled off a sticky note that was prominently taped to a pair of black briefs.

Call me at the office with your schedule. You shouldn't go out alone.

A.

P.S. Dryer broken again. Will call repairman.

"Damn!" she exclaimed loudly. She supposed she should think it sweet that he was concerned but she didn't. No one was going to hover over her and tell her what she could and couldn't do. Especially not Alex. Quickly, she located a pencil and wrote a note of her own.

I can take care of myself.

                                                            G.

P.S. Next time go to the Laundromat.

Again, Gretchen faced the drying rack full of Alex's underwear. If she wanted to take a shower, she had no choice except to move it. She grabbed an armload of matching T-shirts and colored briefs, then tugged at a pair of printed boxer shorts that caught on the end of the rack. Pretty tough stuff for a yuppie dentist, she thought as she held up the shorts and looked at the blue and green paisley print. She'd never found anything especially sexy about men's underwear, but this particular underwear.... She snatched a final pair of royal-blue briefs from the bar and carried the whole armload to Alex's bedroom. She was not going to indulge in fantasies about his underwear.

After dropping the clothes on his bed, Gretchen stopped to look around. She hadn't been in the room since Alex had moved in. She'd carefully avoided it. But now that she was there, she was curious. His room had a solid, masculine air about it. Teakwood shelves filled with books and stereo equipment covered one wall with the bed extending out from the center. The spread was a contemporary design in mellow earth tones, and the windows were covered with matching draperies. His room looked more together after a few weeks than hers had after several months, she noticed as she wandered toward the dresser.

The dresser top was cluttered with a collection of typical male sundries: some loose change, a few gasoline credit card slips, an odd key, a class ring, a pair of ticket stubs from a popular play. Suddenly Gretchen backed away. Feeling very much like an intruder, she hurried out of the bedroom, closing the door behind her. Alex's personal life was none of her business. After all, that was effectively what she'd just finished telling him about herself.

Gretchen's thoughts vacillated between Alex and her money worries all the time she was getting ready for work, but she didn't come up with any answers.

"You don't look so good," Trudy told her when they met on the stairs.

"Thanks a lot," Gretchen answered. "Just what I needed to hear."

"You're not going to like this, either," Trudy added. "The man from the pawnshop was hanging around again last night."

"That's just great." Gretchen dropped her costume bag and sat on the top stair with her chin in her hands. "He found me at the party where I was working. I don't know what would have happened if Alex hadn't been there."

"Alex was there?"

"Yeah," Gretchen replied. "And I ended up telling Alex about the loan, which was another big mistake. He asked if I'd considered borrowing the money from the bank, like I was some sort of dummy. I'm going to have to come up with that payment I missed plus the one for this week." She looked hopefully at Trudy. "You got any ideas?"

Trudy nodded. "Maybe I do. The guy who owns that gas station across the street is an old friend of mine. He told me once if I was ever really up against it he'd let me use his water and hoses to run a car wash. It wouldn't make a lot of money, but on a Saturday morning, if we really hustled—"

"Trudy, that's a great idea. We could take my vacuum and clean the cars inside and out. We could maybe do fifteen cars an hour and at five dollars a car divided by two . . ."

"Not divided by two," Trudy interrupted. "This one's for Joyce. Maybe I can find some more people who'd like to pitch in. I'll ask around the hospital."

"Thanks, Trudy. You're a real friend." Gretchen grabbed her costume bag and hurried down the stairs. She wasn't tired any more. In fact, she felt better than she had for a week.

ALEX WAITED ALL DAY to hear from Gretchen. By late afternoon, every time he approached the reception desk, the receptionist said: "Sorry, Dr. Carson, no calls yet." When he got home and found Gretchen's note, he wadded it into a ball. The hell she could take care of herself. He was checking her schedule when the phone rang.

"So your girlfriend's not answering her phone these days."

Alex immediately recognized the gravelly voice. His grip on the phone tightened. "Stay away from her," he warned.

"She owes me. You tell her it's time to pay up."

Alex slammed down the phone and grabbed his jacket. Gretchen didn't seem to understand how much trouble she was really in.

Gretchen had two parties that night and Alex was at both of them, hanging back in the shadows and slipping away before she left. He could tell she was nervous by the way her eyes darted around the room. Obviously she did need his help, even if she was too bullheaded to admit it. He still couldn't figure out how someone as smart as Gretchen had allowed herself to get into such a stupid mess. But the issue now was getting her out. He knew he could probably come up with the money she'd borrowed if he thought about it for awhile. In the meantime he'd just have to stick with her.

Alex managed to follow Gretchen every night that week without her suspecting anything. By Saturday morning, when a loud clanking woke him up, he was so tired he could hardly move. He turned over to go back to sleep. The high-pitched whine of the vacuum outside his door jolted him out of bed. Angrily he pulled on his robe. The vacuum was winding down as he jerked open the bedroom door.

"What do you think you're doing?" he demanded of Gretchen, who was unpluging the vacuum cord.

"Good morning, Alex," she answered cheerfully. "I didn't wake you, did I?"

He rubbed his eyes. "What time is it?"

"Almost seven. Considering you've been sound asleep every night this week when I got home, I assumed you were probably out jogging by now."

"Well, I'm not," Alex replied gruffly.

"Oh, dear," Gretchen said without any tinge of remorse. "Well, at least the vacuum isn't any louder than your food processor."

He scowled at Gretchen. If she only knew how little sleep he'd really had, maybe she would be more considerate. On the other hand, if she ever found out he'd been following her, she'd be mad as hell. He rubbed his eyes again and focused on Gretchen. She was wearing a bright red turtleneck shirt and skintight black pants. She looked gorgeous—no, *delicious* was a far better description. Actually, he'd like to take her right back to bed with him. But he had the distinct feeling she had other things on her mind, and apparently one of them was cleaning the apartment. "Gretchen," he asked wearily, "why do you have this pressing need to know if the vacuum works at seven o'clock on a Saturday morning?"

"Because I need it for the car wash."

"The car wash?"

"The one Trudy and I are having right across the street." Gretchen picked up the vacuum in one hand and a bucket filled with rags in the other. "All I have left to do is make the signs."

Alex followed her into the kitchen. "I won't ask," he muttered to himself. "I won't ask." The table was stacked with sheets of poster board and an assortment of colored marking pens. He glanced at the empty coffeepot on the counter. "You could have at least made some coffee," he complained.

"Didn't have time," Gretchen said around a bite of cereal. "Gotta get the signs done and meet Trudy in ten minutes."

Alex rinsed out the coffee decanter and took a filter out of the cabinet. He didn't understand how anyone could not have time to make the morning coffee. He glanced over his shoulder at Gretchen, who had put her cereal aside and was printing "Car Wash" in big letters on the sign. He watched her carefully block out the letters until he couldn't contain his curiosity any longer.

"Gretchen, why are you having a car wash?" he finally asked.

"To make money," she answered without looking up.

"You're not going to make any money that way," he protested.

"Don't bet on it. And don't lecture me about the loan, either," she said as she changed from a red marker to a green one. "I don't want to hear it."

Chagrined, Alex didn't answer. He had been pretty tough on her, but borrowing the money like that had been such an asinine move. He walked over to the table. "Maybe you'd make more money if you put something on there about why you're having the car wash."

"Right!" Gretchen dropped the first sign on the floor and started on a second. "I suppose you want me to write 'Money needed to pay off loan shark.' I can see it now."

"No," Alex answered, "I've got a better idea. Give me a piece of poster board and some markers."

Gretchen gave him the supplies more to shut him up than anything else. She ignored the little ripples she felt when he brushed against her shoulder. No time for those feelings. She was in a hurry. Alex didn't seem to understand that, either. He was really rather dense sometimes. Gretchen was still finishing the second sign when Alex held his up for her to look at. The printing was at an angle, and the first line practically ran off the page, but Gretchen's eyes widened with respect.

"You've got it—that's great," she exclaimed, reading the sign again.

Keep a future doctor in school!
Let us
WASH YOUR CAR!!

"Quick, help me make another one." She took out a clean piece of poster board.

"This way, you may even get some donations," he said as he leaned over the table beside her. He quickly began printing, but Gretchen stopped. He was too close. His shoulder was against hers. His cheek, with its morning growth of beard, was very close to her mouth. She licked her lips and suddenly sprang out of the chair. If she stayed there one moment longer, there might not be any car wash.

Alex stopped printing. "Gretchen, what's the matter?"

"Nothing," she lied. "I just thought I'd get a cup of coffee."

"Get me one, too, will you?"

"Sure." She'd gladly get him coffee, anything to stay away from him. She watched his progress from across the kitchen, waiting until he was finished to hand him his coffee mug. "I've really got to go," she said, glancing up at the clock. "Trudy will think I've abandoned her."

"Good luck," Alex said as he took a large drink of his coffee.

"Thanks—and thanks for the signs," Gretchen called to him. She scooped up the vacuum in one hand and the bucket of rags and the signs in the other and hurried out. Even though he made her furious sometimes, Alex did have his moments, Gretchen decided. Actually, sometimes, he was really very nice.

As Gretchen had suspected, Trudy was waiting at the gas station. "Great signs," she said, taking them from under Gretchen's arm.

"And great weather," Gretchen said, glancing at the early morning sun rising against a clear blue sky. "We've got everything going for us. Now let's hope this works."

Within an hour cars were lined up along a side street adjacent to the gas station, and Gretchen and Trudy were washing as fast as they could with the help of two other off-duty nurses and a lab technician Trudy had recruited from the hospital. Several drivers paid them ten dollars instead of five, a few gave them twenties, and one man donated a hundred-dollar bill, saying the country needed good young doctors and he wanted to help.

Gretchen was just finishing a gray Mercedes when she heard Alex's voice behind her. "Looks like you're doing all right. Maybe you *can* make money washing cars."

"Alex, I can hardly believe it," she said, giving the Mercedes' fender a final wipe. "Your signs really paid off."

"Good." He smiled and brushed his hand across her shoulder. "How about calling it a day and going out to lunch? I've got some time before I have to be at the office."

Gretchen accepted a folded bill from the man in the Mercedes. "Good luck with your doctor," he said as he drove off. Opening the bill, she found she was holding fifty dollars.

She stared at it for a moment, then stuffed it into her pocket. "I'm sorry, Alex, I can't go." She met his eyes, willing him to understand. "I've only got two more hours before I have to be Clara the Clown at the hospital and I need to stay here and work."

Alex reached out and touched Gretchen's cheek. "Another time, then."

She watched him walk away, wishing she could go with him, although she knew it would make no sense. She had a gold mine going. She couldn't give up yet.

"You seem to be getting a lot more chummy with your dentist friend," Trudy observed as she handed Gretchen a paper cup of soda.

"You mean Alex?"

"How many dentists are you living with?"

"I'm not really living with him," Gretchen protested.

"You could have fooled me," Trudy shot back. "Have you noticed the way he looks at you?"

Gretchen took a large gulp of soda.

"Obviously you have," Trudy determined. "Have you been to bed with him yet?"

"Of course not! I haven't even been out on a date with him."

"I assume you're prepared. Sex is coming, and probably soon," Trudy predicted.

"Don't be ridiculous. Alex is just a friend."

"He's a gorgeous hunk who is sharing your kitchen and your bathroom and sleeping just down the hall." Trudy crushed her own soda cup and dropped it in the trash. "Don't tell me sex with him has never occurred to you— you'd have to be made of marble to make me believe that. And after the way he was looking at you, I *know* what he was thinking."

"You've got it all wrong, Trudy—"

"You want to do this Corvette or shall I?" Trudy nodded toward a sleek black Corvette that was pulling in.

"Trudy, wait a minute. Stop. That's him. That's Lew."

"You mean the guy you borrowed the money from?"

Gretchen nodded.

"So pay him," Trudy said. "Don't be afraid of him, Gretchen. Do you think you have enough money?"

"Maybe." Gretchen pulled a fistful of bills out of her pocket and quickly counted. The total came to three hundred and five dollars. Drawing a deep breath, she walked over to the man in the car and thrust the bills through the open window. "Here, take it," she said. "That's three hundred and five dollars. Now we're even and you can leave me alone."

"Not quite, lady. It costs you a hundred extra if you're late. That means you got ninety-five to go."

"That's not fair! I already paid you!"

Lew's eyes narrowed as he pocketed the money. "You don't like the penalty—don't be late. I'll come back for the rest later." He stepped hard on the accelerator, spraying Gretchen with a puddle of soapy water as he pulled away.

Trudy put a comforting hand on her shoulder. "Just a few more cars and you'll have enough."

"But then there's next week, and the next—"

"One payment at a time," Trudy counseled. "You never know when lightning will strike or you'll win the lottery."

"I suppose not," Gretchen agreed. "All right, one payment at a time." She picked up a hose and began rinsing another car.

8

ALEX COULD BARELY SEE the little girl tucked into the hospital bed on the far side of the room. He wouldn't have been sure she was there if it hadn't been for the red helium-filled balloon bouncing in the air above her.

"Susan?" he said softly as he approached.

She turned at the sound. She was lying amidst a maze of tubes and monitors, her face pale against the white sheets, her eyes dark and quiet, not full of mischief the way they had been when he last saw her.

"Hi, Dr. Carson."

At least the voice sounded lively, Alex thought. He made his way around the bed and leaned against the windowsill.

"I thought you might be Clara the Clown coming back." Susan pulled a red balloon down to the bed and let it pop back toward the ceiling. "Do you know Clara very well?"

"Yes, Clara's my friend," Alex answered. He thought about how hard it was for Gretchen to see Susan like this and how much of a buffer the clown costume was. Yet Gretchen had done fine the day she had come with him.

"Clara's my friend, too," Susan said. "She comes to see me every Saturday, and we play checkers. Did you ever play checkers with Clara?"

"No," Alex said, "I don't believe I have." He'd never done much of anything with Gretchen just for fun, and it was time to remedy that.

"Clara's not very good," Susan confided. "I always win. I don't think she likes to take my kings."

Alex laughed. "You're probably right. Clowns are better at giving things away. And that's more fun, anyway," he added, pulling a brightly wrapped package from behind his back.

"Neato," Susan exclaimed as she uncovered an electronic Space-Zapper game with dual controls and an assortment of flashing colored lights. "It's a one player and a two player," she announced as she examined it. "I never knew anybody who really had one of these. Will you do it with me?"

"For a little while," Alex agreed. He stayed another few minutes but he could tell that although Susan was trying hard to hide it, she was very tired. "It's time for me to go, Susan," he said, standing up. "But I'll be back and maybe I'll bring Gretchen with me again."

"I like Gretchen, too." Susan looked directly at Alex, her big brown eyes deep and serious. "Gretchen and Clara are a lot like each other, aren't they?"

"Yes," Alex agreed, "they are very much alike." After giving her a quick hug, he wandered downstairs, planning to stop at the reception desk to find out whether Gretchen was still at the hospital. He knew she was probably on her way to another job, but at least he'd say hello to her. On his way, he met Trudy Munson, carrying a box of syringes.

"Alex Carson. What are you doing at the hospital?" she asked him.

"I stopped by to visit Susan Halvorsen."

"Oh, yes, the little girl in 4-B. Gretchen's talked about her."

"Have you seen Gretchen?" Alex asked.

"Nope, but Clara the Clown disappeared into that bathroom a few minutes ago. She'll no doubt emerge as Gretchen in one of her other garbs, unless you two have plans—"

Alex shook his head. "She's never home long enough for me to ask her out."

"Keep trying," Trudy suggested. "I have an idea Gretchen would like to spend time with you, too." She grinned and hurried off down the hall.

Alex paced outside the bathroom for about ten minutes. If Gretchen wanted to spend time with him why couldn't she arrange her schedule to have an evening off? They could have dinner and then maybe catch a movie or a play. She'd said she'd like to go out with him on her next free evening. But as long as she had to pay off the loan, there weren't going to be any free evenings. He could see that very clearly whether she could or not. And the loan had six months to run, she'd said. He wasn't going to wait six months.

The door to the bathroom opened and Alex tensed. Then he caught his breath as Gretchen emerged wearing a belly-dancer costume he had never seen before. Only her eyes, exotically made up, showed above the top of the silky green veil that covered the rest of her face and all her blond hair. A delicate chain of gold coins caressed her forehead. A spangled gold top enhanced her curves and left her torso bare above the sheer green pants that flowed from a snug hip yoke. The yoke was trimmed with more gold coins that swayed as she walked, emphasizing every movement with a soft, bell-like sound.

"Gretchen—" Alex walked toward her, swallowing hard, balancing the woman he knew against the woman he saw. Either way, he longed to touch her.

"Alex, I didn't expect to see you here."

He couldn't stop looking at her. Those eyes. With the veil covering the rest of her face, he was captivated by those huge blue eyes. He swallowed again. "I stopped by to see Susan and thought I'd say hello before you went to work."

"That was nice of you. I was just on my way to the car." She set down her costume bag and started to put on her coat. She was really glad to see him.

"Let me help you," Alex offered. He took the coat and stepped behind her. The harem top left her shoulders bare. He touched the creamy white skin with his fingertips and felt her muscles tense. The last time he'd touched her like that, she'd been in the bathtub and he'd indulged in a slippery, wet exploration that had led his fingers around those soft curves. Alex shuddered and removed his hand.

Gretchen stood motionless, resisting the desire to turn around. Every time he got near her, she felt the same way. But she couldn't—they couldn't—not here in the hospital corridor with all these people. She summoned all her willpower and said softly, "I think I should put on my coat."

Alex noticed that her voice sounded strange. He licked his lips with the tip of his tongue and didn't try to answer, instead forcing himself to hold her coat between them. She fumbled with the sleeves until he took her hand to help her find the opening. Her palm was moist and warm, very much like his own. A nurse pushing a medication cart rounded the corner and Gretchen stepped back. The full, firm flesh beneath these harem pants pressed against Alex and he instinctively pushed back. She stayed against him a few moments more than was absolutely necessary.

"Do you have to work late tonight?" he asked as he picked up the costume bag for her. She seemed to be hugging her coat tightly around herself in a way that reminded him of that night in the kitchen when she had worn it. She hadn't been covering herself up then because she was cold, and that wasn't why she was clutching her coat closed now.

"I've got three parties," she answered, realizing she had to pull away from him. She couldn't go out, as much as she wanted to. "And I have a full schedule tomorrow," she added.

"You can't work all the time, Gretchen." He held the hospital door open for her, easing back as her shoulder brushed his.

"I don't have any choice. I made the back loan payment this morning, but I've got to come up with another three hundred dollars by Wednesday."

"I'll make you a deal. I'll pay the rent if you'll go out with me Friday night."

"I forgot about the rent," she gasped.

"I just told you I'll pay it."

"You do that, Yuppie, but I still can't go out with you. I'm booked Friday."

"How about Saturday?"

"Yep. Booked then, too."

"The following Friday?"

"You don't give up, do you?"

He opened the door of her Volkswagen, tossed the costume bag inside and stepped back so she could get in. "Don't you want to go out with me, Gretchen?"

She hesitated, and instead of getting into the car she turned her back to the door and faced him. Her eyes reflected frustration and desire. "You can't imagine how much I'd like to go. Maybe the Friday after next."

He took a step closer. Her coat had fallen open and he wanted to touch her. "Are you sure we have to wait that long?" He slid his hand inside her coat and felt her quiver as he touched the bare skin at her waist. "It seems like forever," he whispered.

"I know," she answered. "But I can't this weekend."

His other hand found its way under the edge of the harem veil and unfastened it. The silky material slid off, exposing the rest of her face. Her lips were full, pink and moist and probably warm, begging to be kissed. His fingers caressed the curve of her cheek, and she gasped softly.

A station wagon pulled into an empty space in the next row. Alex moved sideways until his body blocked the driver's view. "I really wish you didn't have to work tonight," he told her.

"So do I."

Inside her coat he stroked the fullness of her breast. "Are you sure you can't call in sick?"

A woman in a nurse's uniform got out of the station wagon and hurried past them toward the hospital. Alex leaned closer to Gretchen, bending his head against hers. Above the dangling gold chain earrings, her earlobe was a soft oval. He flicked it lightly with his tongue.

"I have to go to work, Alex."

He could smell the light scent of perfume in her hair. Her lower body pressed against him, and he pushed her tight against the car, throbbing against her. "Gretchen, don't go," he whispered.

"There's no one to fill in for me. I'm afraid if I don't go, I'll lose my job."

He heard the quiet desperation and sensed the battle raging inside her. In that moment he knew he could make her stay and he almost did. But she'd regret it later. He tried not to care, but he did care and it was getting in the way. Slowly his hands moved to her waist and then behind her back. He held her body tight against his for one moment more before he let her go.

"No, Alex, don't kiss me," she said as he leaned down toward her. Quickly she slipped into the car.

"I'll see you when you get home," he told her. He wasn't sure he could wait that long.

"It'll be late."

"I don't care how late it is." He slammed the door and watched her drive away. Turning abruptly, he walked across the parking lot to the Porsche.

GRETCHEN THOUGHT ABOUT ALEX all afternoon. Something had happened to their roommate relationship. Something very specific. Every time she got near him she had only one thing on her mind, and the feeling was obviously mutual. She thought about Trudy's warning, but Trudy was probably just guessing. Surely there wasn't anything so telling about the way Alex looked at her. On the other hand, there hadn't been much question about how either one of them felt when they were leaning against that car in the hospital parking lot.

Those feelings hadn't subsided much by the time Gretchen arrived home well after midnight. Logic told her she was being ridiculous. The message her body gave her said something else. The lights were on when she opened the door, but everything was quiet except for the steady hum of the pump in the fish tank. He'd told her he would be waiting for her. She checked his bedroom. The bed was still made. The kitchen was empty. Her bedroom was dark.

Wandering into the living room, she stopped, smiling. Alex was sound asleep on the couch, a book closed over his hand. He'd obviously been lying there reading while he waited for her, and he had simply fallen asleep. Kneeling down beside him, she listened to his deep, easy breathing and considered waking him. He'd probably take her to bed with him if she did. She even raised her hand to touch his cheek, but then she pulled back. She studied his face—the firm jaw, the straight nose, the eyelashes longer and darker than any man deserved. She couldn't deny the attraction. It had been creeping up on them from the very beginning. But in her heart of hearts she wasn't sure she really was ready to act on it.

With Alex Carson she could have no one-night stand. He lived with her. She'd have to face him the next day, and the next, and the day after that. Sure, sex was fun. But sex led to involvement. Maybe not for some people, but it did for her. And how could she, Gretchen Bauer, even consider getting seriously involved with a yuppie dentist who ate health food and drove a Porsche? He was part of another world.

Gretchen stood up. She'd been working too hard. It was time to go to bed—alone.

ALEX WAS DREAMING when he woke up. It was a wonderful sensuous dream about a woman with soft blond hair nuzzling up against him and stroking his thighs, her hands moving in tiny circles expanding outward farther and farther. Abruptly Alex opened his eyes. Light was streaming in the window. He sat up, checked his watch and groaned. It was morning; he was stiff and sore from a night on the couch; and either Gretchen hadn't come home or he'd slept through it. Impossible, he decided, slowly standing up. He couldn't have slept that soundly.

He quietly opened her bedroom door and found her curled up with her quilt, her T-shirt barely covering her backside. "Damn," he muttered softly. Those late nights all week had taken their toll. She'd managed to come in and get ready for bed and he hadn't heard a thing. He stepped into her room, but she didn't wake up. What he wanted to do was get in bed with her. The temptation was almost overwhelming. She stirred in her sleep, and Alex noted that he'd been right. She did wear the lacy white panties under the T-shirt. As he watched her, he imagined her body coming alive out of the softness of sleep, her lips ripe and delicious on his, the feeling of her flesh beneath his hands, his mouth....

Decisively, Alex backed out of Gretchen's bedroom and closed the door. He had no qualms about cancelling his nine o'clock appointment with the contractor to discuss his condominium, even though the date had been set for a month. Nor would he have minded in the least calling Ed to cancel their tennis game and the dinner at his house that was to follow. But he would mind a hell of a lot if he went to Gretchen and she said no. That had happened before. When they had sex, he was going to be damned sure she wanted it as much as he did.

Alex walked into the bathroom, picked up the pencil and pad of sticky notes that had become a permanent fixture beside the Water Pik. Once his message was completed, he smacked the paper against the mirror, stepped into the shower and turned on the cold water.

GRETCHEN FOUND THE NOTE around noon the next day, just after she woke up.

Where do you want to go a week from Friday?

A.

P.S. Why didn't you wake me?

She smiled and quickly answered with a note of her own. She frankly didn't care where they went as long as it wasn't a bachelor party and there were no helium balloons in sight.

I don't know. You choose.

G.

P.S. *Modern Etiquette* page 233.
Rule #1. Never wake a sleeping yuppie.

The following morning she got an answer, and this time she laughed out loud.

We will dine at an exquisite French restaurant and go dancing afterward.

A.

P.S. Smart ass.

Sometimes she had to remind herself that Alex was a stodgy yuppie dentist, because he kept getting out of character. Dinner and dancing sounded fantastic, but what was she going to wear? Gretchen stuck the note on the faucet handle and leaned down to wash her face. Pants were out. So were skirts and sweaters. She couldn't steal from a costume because he'd seen all those. That pretty much took care of her wardrobe. She blotted her face dry with a thick towel and pondered the note again. Obviously she couldn't buy a dress, not on her budget. That left only one option. It was her turn to eat crow.

Ten minutes later, dressed in sweats and carrying a glass of iced tea, she knocked on Trudy's door.

"Hi, Trudy," she said as the door opened. "May I come in?"

"You've got a problem. I can see it."

"No, actually, well, I just thought I'd stop by and see how you were." Gretchen followed Trudy into a kitchen almost identical to her own and sat down at the table.

Trudy eyed her suspiciously. "Is it money? Has Lew been after you again?"

"No, honest," Gretchen assured her. "I've already got the money to pay this week and I'm working on the next payment."

"All that and half the rent to boot? What did you do— win the lottery?"

"Hardly," Gretchen answered. "Actually, Alex offered to pay the rent," she admitted.

"Oh, I see." Trudy shot Gretchen a meaningful glance.

"No, you don't. He just happens to be solvent at the moment, and I'm not. Besides, his junk takes up three-quarters of the space so he should pay more," Gretchen added defensively.

Trudy filled her mug with coffee and picked up her pack of cigarettes from the counter. "So you're fresh out of problems and just stopped by to chat," she observed. "That's a first."

Gretchen hesitated. She couldn't seem to find any graceful way to ease into what she'd come to ask. "Well, there is one thing," she began slowly.

Trudy smiled and lit a cigarette.

"You know that dress you bought at the thrift shop?" Gretchen avoided Trudy's eyes. She absolutely hated having to do this.

"Dress?" Trudy echoed innocently.

"You know, the red one." Trudy obviously wasn't going to make this easy.

"Oh, the red silk one? You mean the size four?"

Gretchen gave her what she hoped was a withering look, but Trudy only smiled placidly. "Yes, dammit, the red silk, size four," Gretchen said. "You know very well what dress I mean."

"Just wanted to be sure I had the right one. What did you want to know about the red silk dress, size four that looked absolutely ravishing on this friend of mine who was too proud to buy it because it came from the thrift shop?"

"Well, Alex invited me out to dinner a week from Friday—" Gretchen saw the smug expression on Trudy's face and banged her iced-tea glass on the table. "Come on, Trudy, cut it out. Did you get the dress dry-cleaned?"

Trudy burst out laughing. "You've got to admit, you deserved to squirm a little bit. Of course I had it cleaned and I picked it up yesterday. It is absolutely the most gorgeous creation I've ever seen."

Gretchen sighed with relief. "As much as I hate to admit it, I'd be up a creek if you hadn't insisted on buying that dress."

Trudy took a final drag of her cigarette and crushed it out in a small skillet-shaped ashtray. "I assume this anticipated outing signals a new phase in a budding relationship?"

"Frankly, I don't know what it signals. Alex came to the hospital Saturday and I talked to him for a few minutes before I went to work."

"So? You're living with him. I assume you talk to him on a regular basis."

"Well, I do talk to him sometimes, except we're not home together much." Gretchen realized she wasn't making much sense. "Come on, Trudy, don't make this hard, too. Something different is happening with Alex and me— maybe not different, exactly, just more."

"So you went to bed with him." Trudy lit another cigarette.

"No, that's not what I said."

"What you said, whether you meant to or not, was that you're going to have sex but haven't quite admitted it to yourself yet."

Gretchen stared at her iced tea. "Since when did you become the resident psychologist?"

"Every nurse is a psychologist. It goes with the job."

"Just like being blunt about things like sex." Gretchen finished her iced tea, wishing she could change the course of their conversation to something easier, like the weather.

Trudy laughed. "Subtlety was never my thing. It causes too many misunderstandings." She walked over to the counter to refill her coffee mug. "Now, let's go get this gorgeous red silk, size four."

Once Gretchen saw the dress freshly cleaned, she had to agree that it looked like something directly out of a fashionable boutique.

"I told you it was gorgeous," Trudy gloated after Gretchen put on the dress. "And a perfect fit. Now, aren't you glad I bought it?"

"Okay, okay, you win," Gretchen agreed. She smiled at her image in the mirror. No one would ever guess where the dress came from and, she decided, if she tried hard, she could forget, too.

After thanking Trudy, she took the dress home and hung it in the back of her closet, pushing the rest of her clothes to the sides so the delicate silk wouldn't get wrinkled. Only a little more than a week till she could wear it. That problem was solved.

A few days later Gretchen passed through the corner drugstore to get a lipstick to match her dress. After selecting one a shade lighter than the fabric she had snipped from the seam, she picked up a hand basket and checked her list: toothpaste, deodorant, lottery ticket.... She quickly found the deodorant and then started up an adjacent aisle to get the toothpaste. Why couldn't Alex supply toothpaste free from his office? He provided dental floss. She was heading toward the cashier at the back of the store where she could get her lottery ticket when she nearly ran into a sensuous poster of a lithe couple running hand in hand on a moonlit beach. Across the top of the picture were the words: "For those moments of love..."

Gretchen stopped. She was face-to-face with rows and shelves of condoms. Thick, thin, natural, latex, colored, transparent, ribbed.... Ribbed? She reached for a flowered package and studied it carefully. If she did have sex with Alex, she needed to be sure they were prepared. But by the time she had read the descriptions on a dozen or so brands of condoms, she was thoroughly confused. Didn't most men have their favorites? Surely Alex would take care of it. Finally, just to be safe, she selected a pink package of condoms, shoved it under the toothpaste in her basket and went to the pharmacy cash register at the back of the store to pay for her purchases.

ALEX WALKED into the drugstore with a specific purpose in mind. He stood in front of the condom display shaking his head. Why would anyone think a poster like that would sell condoms? Perfume, maybe, but not condoms. Condoms were male items, direct and basic. He scanned the shelves. So many different kinds out now—all these pastel colors and flowers on the packages. No man would buy something that came in a flowered box. He picked up a package of Trojans and headed for the cashier at the front of the store. Then he remembered he also needed shaving cream, which was near the back register. He rounded the end of the aisle and stopped short.

"Alex!" Gretchen gasped in surprise.

"Gretchen! I didn't expect to run into you here." He eased the package of condoms into his jacket pocket, hoping no one would notice and accuse him of shoplifting.

"I was just picking up a lottery ticket." Gretchen was sure he could see through the small brown bag she held. Quickly selecting her numbers, she paid for the ticket and turned toward the door.

"I'd offer you a ride home, but I rode my bike," Alex apologized.

"That's all right. It's a beautiful day for a walk." Grateful to escape, Gretchen left the drugstore.

Relieved, Alex watched her go and took the package of Trojans out of his pocket. Damned good thing he'd come on his bike. Not that condoms were any secret. Everybody used them, and these days buying a pack of condoms wasn't much different from buying a tube of toothpaste. But he still didn't want Gretchen with him when he did it. He paid for the condoms and went outside to unlock his bike. He was halfway home before he remembered that he hadn't bought the shaving cream.

When Gretchen got home, she stuffed the pink box of condoms into the top drawer of her bedside table and tried to forget they were there. But every night when she set her alarm clock she remembered. And every night after she closed her eyes, she tossed restlessly, neither asleep nor awake, feeling Alex's lips on hers, his breath warm against her ear. On Wednesday morning, or more correctly early afternoon, she stumbled sleepily into the bathroom and found a note on the mirror. With a yawn she pulled it off and read:

Pet store closed yesterday. Meetings today. Out of birdseed. Can you drop some by the office on your way to work? Thanks.

A.

Gretchen stared at the note as if it was an alien being. She wouldn't have minded doing Alex a favor. She wouldn't even have been upset because the favor required driving ten miles out of her way to stop at his office. But this—this was too much!

"He's sending me to buy birdseed? For his mother's stupid canary?" Gretchen fumed out loud. "He expects me to waste what little free time I have on that dumb bird." She didn't even know what the thing ate. Obviously something expensive. She pulled down the ten-dollar bill Alex had left taped to the mirror. What a waste of money, she thought, stuffing the bill into her purse.

Gretchen was still irritated as she pulled the Volkswagen into the only parking place she could find and carried the bag of birdseed two blocks to Alex's office. When she got there, the door was locked, but she could hear Tweety inside trilling lustily. That would really fix it, she decided, pounding on the door, if she'd come all this way to bring him birdseed and he wasn't even here....

The latch rattled and Alex opened the door. "Gretchen, come in," he said stepping aside. "What are you doing here?"

"What do you mean, what am I doing here?" she retorted. "I brought your dumb birdseed, and I want you to know it took me almost an hour in an already cram-packed day to do it." She thrust the bag into his hands and then she took a good look at him in his light blue clinic jacket. "My God, Alex!" she exclaimed. "You look like a dentist."

"What did you expect me to look like?" he shot back. "I am a dentist."

"But you usually don't look like one." She glanced around the empty waiting room. "If you don't have any patients, why didn't you go buy your own birdseed?"

Splitting open the bag with his thumb, Alex walked over to fill Tweety's food tray. "Because there's a dental meeting the first Wednesday of the month, but this one was canceled at the last minute. I tried to phone but you must have already left the apartment." He set the bag of birdseed under the table and turned to Gretchen. Her eyes were sultry and heavily outlined with the exotic makeup he remembered from her belly-dancer costume. He glanced down at the sheer green harem pants beneath her long coat and knew she was wearing his favorite costume. He put his hands on her shoulders and grinned. "Now, if you'll quit being angry about the birdseed—which I do appreciate and so does Tweety—I'll show you around the office."

"Thanks, but no thanks," Gretchen answered. Shrugging away his hands and trying to ignore the sensations they left even through her coat, she started for the door. "I hate dentists' offices. Remember?"

"Hold it!" Not wanting her to leave, Alex caught her arm. "When was the last time you were in a dentist's office? Any dentist's office?"

Gretchen thought hard. "I don't remember. Let me go."

Alex spun her around and held both arms. "When do you have to be at work?"

"Not until five, but I've got to run a dozen errands and—"

"And see the dentist," Alex finished for her.

"No, absolutely not." Her eyes flashed defiantly. She might stay for other reasons, but she was not going to have her teeth examined.

"Now, Gretchen." He slid one hand across the back of her neck under her hair. "It's not every day you get an offer of free dental work."

"I don't need any dental work." She clamped down her mouth shut. She should have told him she had to go to work immediately. Then he'd have let her alone. But she wouldn't have liked that, either. For some insane reason she didn't want to go.

He studied her carefully. "You really are afraid, aren't you?"

"Of course not," she lied. "I'm just in a hurry."

"Gretchen, I won't hurt you." His fingers gently kneaded the back of her neck. "I won't even do any work on your teeth unless you want me to."

She eyed him dubiously. His fingers were wonderfully warm, but she mustn't let that distract her. "Maybe some other time," she answered.

Slowly he let go of her arm and touched her cheek. "Why not right now? I'll show you our special examining room."

"I don't know, Alex." He had taken hold of her hand and she was following him. "I really don't want to do this—"

She stopped at the door of examining room three. In the dim light she was sure it was a fantasy. Everything was a deep, dark blue and suspended from the ceiling, were myriad tiny silver stars. Hundreds and hundreds of silver stars floating in space. "Alex, what's this?"

"I tell the kids that this room is whatever they want it to be. Usually their imaginations are so busy, they hardly notice what I'm doing."

Entranced, Gretchen walked inside, almost as if she were drawn by the power of a full moon that glowed from the end of the room.

"Let me take your coat," Alex offered, "and I'll have a quick look in your mouth."

"You're just going to look—nothing else," she declared as she lay back in the reclining chair and gazed at the stars floating above her.

9

THE MOMENT ALEX LOOKED DOWN at her, he knew he wasn't going to examine her teeth. He wasn't even going to try. "Gretchen," he said softly. Her blue eyes were wide. He tried to focus only on them.

"Yes?"

Despite his best efforts, his eyes strayed to the soft outline of her high, firm breasts underneath the harem top. He knew she wore nothing under it. He could just slide his hands right down inside and—

"Gretchen," he said in a husky voice, "I think the dentist has left for the day."

She saw his eyes, dark with desire, and she didn't have to ask what he meant. She moved over slightly. "Why don't you sit down? There's plenty of room." She couldn't believe she was saying that, considering the circumstances, but it was what she wanted. She looked up at him as though for the first time. High above, the silver stars were shimmering against the backdrop of deep blue. A tiny shiver ran through her as his fingers toyed with the bottom of her harem top, caressing the warm, fair skin.

"You know," he said, pressing against her hip as he sat beside her, "I like this costume."

Gretchen's eyes took on a mischievous glint. "I don't like *your* costume at all. You just told me the dentist had left for the day." She reached for the button at the top of his clinic jacket.

"I think the patient went with him," Alex said, as she moved down to the second button. His jacket fell open and he took it off and tossed it onto a chair.

"But you do realize I have to go run errands," Gretchen added. She didn't sound convincing even to herself.

"Of course you do," he agreed. "You'll need to leave any minute." Her lips looked just as delicious as they had before, except now he could do something about it. He lowered his mouth to hers, teasing her lips with his tongue. "First, before you go anywhere, I'm going to kiss you."

"Maybe just once," Gretchen murmured as his mouth closed over hers, firm and demanding. She didn't care about her errands any more. She didn't care about anything except kissing Alex. She reached up and put her hands behind his neck, and the kiss grew deeper and more compelling.

She felt his hands moving along the edge of her harem top. Her whole body tensed in anticipation and she gasped softly. She couldn't be doing this. She'd come to bring him birdseed. And he'd enticed her into his office. And there were a dozen other things she really needed to do. His lips explored her neck and shoulders in a trail of feathery kisses. Perhaps those other things weren't so important after all.

Gretchen opened her eyes. "Alex," she murmured, "maybe you should take off your tie."

"Maybe I should." He sat, loosened his tie and pulled it off, then unbuttoned his shirt. His eyes never left hers. "You've been driving me wild, Gretchen." He stroked her soft blond curls. "Every night when I get home the bathroom smells like your dusting powder, and it makes me think about you."

She helped take off his shirt. "And every morning the bathroom smells like your shaving lotion, and once I even looked out around the shower curtain to make sure you weren't there with me."

"You're a very desirable woman, Gretchen," he whispered, pulling her to him. Slowly, he outlined her earlobe with the tip of his tongue. "Did you know your ears are perfect?"

She pulled playfully away. "No, but I know I can't stand it when you do that—" He nuzzled against her ear again and she dodged his lips. "Alex, this is insane. We live together. We could do this at home any time—"

"Are you telling me you want to go home?"

Gretchen didn't answer. She didn't want to go anywhere. With her hands behind his neck, she pulled his mouth down to hers. His lips were wet and possessive, teasing and playing and taking control. She buried her hands in his hair, then ran her fingers across his broad, muscular back until he groaned with pleasure. He kissed her again, and just when she wanted him never to stop, he drew back. His fingers outlined the curve of her breasts above the harem top, and she knew what he was going to do.

"This is the sexiest piece of clothing I've ever seen," Alex confided. "I've wanted to take it off from the first minute I saw you wearing it."

She remembered exactly when that moment had been. "You mean in the hospital corridor? Right there, in front of all those people?"

"Yep." He caught the first hook between his thumb and forefinger. "You felt it, too, Gretchen. Otherwise you wouldn't remember."

"Not necessarily," she murmured, as he unfastened two more hooks. It was true. She'd wanted him then, but not half so much as she wanted him now. She pressed her head back, watching him, feeling her breasts swell as she waited for him.

The last hook slipped free and Alex's gaze swept across her milk-white skin. Then he lowered his head. His mouth played across her breasts and fed the mounting desire in her. As she opened her eyes, the stars were shining above her, and then his mouth found hers, and the coarse hair on his chest pressed against her smooth skin.

"You didn't answer when I asked if you wanted to go home," Alex whispered. He knew her desire matched his own, but he wanted her to say so. The emotion that gripped them had been building for weeks, spilling over in brief encounters when they let their guard down and frequent bickering when they didn't. Now it was almost time. His eyes swept her body from the baby-soft skin of her breasts to her waist, which was so small he could almost span it with his hands. As she lay on her back, the outline of her legs was clearly visible under her sheer pants. He wanted to take those pants off, too. His eyes traveled upward to meet hers. "Do you want to go home, Gretchen?"

"It would make so much more sense."

He put both his hands on her thighs and traced her curves upward to her waist. Gretchen quivered. "That isn't what I asked you," he said in a hoarse voice. "I asked if you wanted to go home."

"I suppose we should." He was sitting with his hip against hers. The button on the waistband of his slacks was directly in her line of vision. She stared at it. He'd be so much more comfortable if that button were unfastened. She stroked the line of dark curls on his chest until it disappeared at his waist. He drew a sharp breath and sucked in his already flat stomach. The waistband was loose, but the fabric below it drew even tighter than before. Gretchen reached for the button and as she pulled it free the zipper below it opened as well.

"I recognize these boxer shorts," she said, remembering them hanging in the bathroom. But as she looked at the blue and green print fabric, her attention was quickly drawn elsewhere. She reached toward him.

Alex moaned softly as she touched him, then gripped her shoulders and drew her up to him. "You've answered my question," he breathed. "We're staying right here." His deep, probing kiss lasted until Gretchen didn't care where they were as long as they were together. And alone. Then, with the last shred of logic she had left, she realized why she'd thought they ought to go home. She remembered the bag from the drugstore stuffed in the drawer of her nightstand, waiting there just in case. "We can't, Alex—" She stopped, not sure how to bring up the subject and not wanting to. "We aren't prepared to—" Her eyes pleaded with him to finish her thought.

"Gretchen—" he began, his voice husky from the passion surging through him. "We are prepared." Her body relaxed against his and he knew the last obstacle was gone. He slipped down her harem pants, running his hands tantalizingly between her thighs and behind her knees and then stopping to kiss her. Beneath the harem pants were the lacy bikini panties he'd seen before on the drying rack. They'd been sexy then, but nothing like this.

Gretchen arched her hips toward him as he caught the panties and pulled them down. She gasped when he touched her. "Oh, Alex, do that again," she whispered.

"Like this?"

Gretchen couldn't answer. Desire churned through her.

"Or maybe like this?"

Alex's mouth was hot and wet and insistent. Gretchen closed her eyes. She could feel his impatience, and when he stopped to take off the rest of his clothes, she sat forward to help him, her hands exploring and slowing him down until he finally muttered in a hoarse voice, "Now, Gretchen, I want you now." He sheathed himself, rising up magnificently, and she held out her arms.

Her hips rose to meet him, and she wrapped her arms and legs around him, drinking in his musky male scent that was now so familiar. He seemed to fill her body, thrusting deeper and deeper and sending pleasure washing through her in great waves. She moved in his rhythm to a final moment when reality shattered as their passion crested together.

As their breathing slowed, she held him against her, thinking she might never get enough of him. When he finally propped his head on his hand and looked at her, his deep brown eyes were gentle. "My God, Gretchen, why did we wait so long?" he asked.

"I don't know, Alex," she answered softly. "I don't think I understand much of anything about this."

He stroked the curve of her breast with his finger. "Then maybe we need to talk about it."

"I don't know if I want to talk about it. We don't make any sense, Alex. It's almost like this is a dream and we're about to wake up."

Alex frowned, not sure what she was trying to say. "We can't go back, you know." He studied her carefully. "You don't want to go back, do you, Gretchen?"

"No, of course not," she answered quickly. "It's just that, well, we're very different kinds of people, Alex, and we're getting sort of involved."

He laughed softly. "I'd say we are involved. Very involved." He flicked her earlobe playfully until she pulled away.

"Alex, stop," she demanded, pushing on his chest. "How can we have a serious discussion when you're doing that?"

"I didn't know we were having a serious discussion." He zeroed in on her ear again until she buried her head in his chest.

"I never should have told you how that affects me," she muttered. "We were talking about getting involved."

"And we agreed that we are, right?"

Ripples of doubt raced through Gretchen. She raised her head abruptly. "Wrong, Yuppie. We agreed that we have some problems to discuss. Our paths would never have crossed at all if you hadn't claimed squatter's rights in my apartment."

"So let's discuss," Alex said amiably.

"Not this afternoon." Gretchen scrambled to a sitting position. "If I don't get dressed and out of here this very instant, I'm going to be late to work."

"That wouldn't be such a crisis." Alex leaned up to kiss her, but Gretchen pushed him away.

"Oh, yes it would." Gretchen scooted off the end of the chair and began to gather her clothes together. "And it's going to be another crisis if I don't get that loan payment in on time. That's part of the reason we're different, Alex, part of what you don't understand."

He sat up and reached for his pants. "Don't underestimate me, Gretchen. I understand more than you think I do."

She finished hooking her harem top and turned to him. "I hope so, Alex, but I just don't know."

GRETCHEN RAN ON AUTOMATIC all that day and the next, thinking about virtually nothing but Alex. When she considered the situation objectively, she could see that it was ridiculous for her to get mixed up with a yuppie dentist. Yet she was having a harder and harder time being objective where Alex was concerned. When she walked into the bathroom Friday morning and found a single red rose on the vanity, just in front of the Water Pik, objectivity deserted her entirely. She smelled the rose's sweet perfume then pulled the note off the vase.

Dear Gretchen,
Thinking about you. See you at eight.

A.

That was all it said, but that was enough. He was looking forward to their date as much as she was. No point in worrying, she decided. She was probably making a big deal out of nothing at all.

ALEX WAS DOING A ROOT CANAL on his last patient and trying hard not to think about his date with Gretchen when his mother called. He was going to have the receptionist take a message until he remembered his mother was in the south of France.

"Is something wrong?" he demanded, grabbing the phone.

Although the connection was so poor that he could barely hear his mother's voice through the crackling static, he quickly determined there was no crisis. She seemed to be telling him she wanted him to turn on the heat in her house and check the place over before she returned the next day. He grudgingly agreed. That meant getting up in the morning and driving out to McLean. But he sure as hell wasn't going tonight. Tonight belonged to Gretchen.

Alex had just finished up and was taking off his gloves when Ed walked in. "I understand your mother called. I hope there's no problem."

"None," Alex assured him. "She's flying back from Europe tonight and she wanted me to check her house, turn on the heat, things like that."

"Does that mean the end of the birdseed all over the waiting room?" Ed asked hopefully.

"You've got it," Alex answered. "Fortunately I drove today so I'll take Tweety home for the night. And the next time my mother takes off on one of her jaunts," Alex added, "somebody else gets the canary. It's sure not going to be Gretchen and me."

Ed raised a curious eyebrow. "Gretchen and me? I take it your love life's looking up."

"Maybe a little."

"That goofy smile is a dead giveaway every time," Ed observed with a chuckle. "How did you manage to get through to her?"

Alex stripped off his clinic jacket and hung it on a hook in the corner. "My natural charm, no doubt," he flipped back.

"Now you're being a smart ass."

Alex grinned. "That's what Gretchen says."

"Oh? What else does Gretchen say?" Ed inquired.

"A whole lot of things, actually." Alex smiled. "She calls me Yuppie."

"Yuppie?" Ed shook his head. "I really am out of touch. In my day, they called you sweetheart. Is there some particular reason she picked Yuppie?"

Alex shrugged. "She's got a hang-up with money."

"Most women do."

"No, hers is different. She's flat broke and really struggling, and she's got the idea I'm rich."

"You mean she's after your money?"

"No, nothing like that. I think she resents it. Gretchen's . . . well, she's unique."

"And she's really gotten to you." Ed clapped him on the back. "From the sound of things, you're in for trouble. All I can do is wish you luck."

Alex thought about Ed's reaction as he pulled the Porsche alongside the curb near the apartment building. Gretchen didn't strike him as trouble. She was a little wacky and she did have herself in a real financial mess, but she seemed to be digging her way out. Of course, she also ate that ghastly sugared cereal and showed no interest whatsoever in health or exercise. But she still seemed to manage to have that tiny waist and curves in all the right places. Alex smiled as he lifted Tweety's cage out of the car. Maybe Gretchen had gotten to him, as Ed put it, and maybe he didn't care.

"Alex?"

He heard Gretchen's voice in the bedroom and quickly set the bird cage on the living room table.

"I'm home," he called.

Gretchen pulled the zipper halfway up the back of the red dress, then smoothed the skirt with her hands. One look in the mirror told her the effect was perfect. She spun around once more, then heard a low whistle from the doorway.

"Wow!" he said softly, staring at her. He'd never seen her like that. In costumes, yes, but they were fantasy. The dress was real, and in it Gretchen was breathtaking. "Turn around," he directed.

"Why?"

Alex shook his head. She was still Gretchen. "Because I want to see if you're as beautiful from the back as you are from the front."

"Oh." She smiled with sudden understanding. "You like my dress."

"Of course I like your dress. Turn around."

She complied, with a flourish, enjoying his admiration.

"Again," he ordered, "but slowly this time."

This time she moved in slow motion, exaggerating each movement, and Alex enjoyed every inch of her. "Absolute perfection," he proclaimed, "except we need to finish the zipper." In two strides he was behind her, planting a kiss on her back. "Just think how fortunate it was that I moved in," he teased. "You'd never be able to manage your zippers without me." Catching the tab, he was about to pull the zipper upward when he noticed the label inside the dress. He recognized the well-known designer immediately.

As he slowly closed the zipper, a thoughtful frown crossed his face. "Gretchen, isn't this a new dress?"

She hesitated. She'd hoped he wouldn't ask that question. "This is the first time I've worn it," she answered carefully.

Alex's frown deepened. She had even less money sense that he'd thought. She already owed a bundle of money, yet she was buying designer dresses. "What did you do, win the lottery?" he asked lightly.

"Don't I wish." She swirled away from him and stepped into a pair of black pumps. "Just imagine, Alex, what it would be like to win more than two and a half million dollars. It would solve everything."

Alex shook his head. Gretchen was a dreamer. "The odds against winning the lottery are astronomical," he replied. "If people saved the money they spend on lottery tickets, they'd be better off."

"You're no fun!" Gretchen exclaimed, relieved that she effectively had led him away from the subject of the dress.

"I'm not, huh?" He took her in his arms and leaned down to kiss her neck.

"Well, maybe—" Gretchen snuggled against him.

"But if I stay here much longer, we're never going to make it to dinner," he whispered.

"You're right," she said, stepping back. "Go get ready while I comb my hair."

Alex showered and shaved quickly and put on a dark suit. He couldn't stop thinking about that dress. He realized he probably should be flattered because she'd bought it to go out with him. But he couldn't get away from the probable price, which was even more outlandish under Gretchen's circumstances. Maybe Ed was right. Maybe he needed to know a whole lot more about Gretchen Bauer before it was too late, if it wasn't already.

When he walked into the living room, Gretchen was sitting in the moss-green chair with her arms folded and a scowl on her face. "Alex, you've brought that stupid bird back again."

"Tweety? He's only temporary." Alex walked over and removed the cage cover.

"How temporary?" she demanded, raising her voice as Tweety tuned up. "I thought I made it clear the last time. I will not live with that canary." Gretchen was so adamant that it even surprised her. She'd never particularly disliked canaries before, but she abhorred this one.

"He'll just be here overnight," Alex assured her. "Mother's coming home tomorrow, so I'm going to take him back and check on the house."

"You're sure?" she asked suspiciously.

"Absolutely," Alex assured her. "Tell you what," he suggested as he held her coat, "why don't you ride along with me tomorrow? The azaleas are coming out and the daffodils are in bloom. It should be a pretty drive."

"Will your mother be there?"

Alex heard the reluctance in her voice. "No, she's not coming in until the afternoon," he answered slowly. "Does that make a difference?"

"I guess not. I'd like to go," she added, trying to sound enthusiastic. But a whole series of queer sensations were bouncing around in her stomach. She didn't want to get mixed up with Alex's mother and Alex's background, which made her wonder whether she really should be getting involved with Alex.

By the time they'd arrived at the restaurant and ordered their hors d'oeuvres, Gretchen had forgotten her misgivings. Alex was a charming date who seemed both able and willing to discuss everything from national politics to contemporary art to the latest trends in fashion. From the wine to the crème brûlée, dinner was delicious, and afterward, when Alex swirled her around the dance floor, Gretchen thought she was in heaven.

"Where did you learn to dance like that?" she asked breathlessly. "Nobody knows how to dance any more, not really dance."

"I had to go to this awful thing called cotillion when I was in junior high school. The boys had to serve the girls punch and we all wore white gloves so we wouldn't have to actually touch skin to skin." He chuckled at the memory. "But after about the third week I discovered dancing was fun, although to this day I've never admitted it to my mother."

"She made you go?"

"Yeah, didn't you have to do things like that?"

Gretchen thought about her life when she was in junior high school. Her father had walked out, Nancy was sick, her mother was working two jobs, and sometimes the only thing to eat for dinner was cereal three days in a row. "No,

Alex," Gretchen said quietly. "I didn't have to take dancing lessons."

"You were lucky." He took her hand. "Would you like another cup of coffee or some brandy?"

"No, thank you, Alex. I think I'm ready to go home."

He signaled the waiter and within minutes they were in the Porsche heading toward the apartment. "You're very quiet," he said taking her hand as they waited at a stop sign.

"I guess life's just a little overwhelming sometimes," she answered.

She didn't want to talk to him about what was bothering her. Actually she wasn't even sure she could put it in words. Their backgrounds really shouldn't matter. That's what her mother had always said. "Don't pay any attention to them," her mother had told her when the other kids teased her about her clothes. "You're as good as any of them and better than most. People are what matters, baby, not things. Don't ever let anyone tell you different."

"I hope I'm not overwhelming," Alex said as he pulled the car into a parking place near the apartment. "I had a good time tonight, Gretchen." He turned toward her and took both her hands. In the glow of the streetlight she could see the intensity in his eyes. "I like to take you out," he continued. "I want to take you dancing again, and to the theater, and maybe some night we can ride the cruise ship along the Potomac."

"Alex, I don't know when I can—"

He got out of the car and walked around to open the door for her. "We'll work something out," he assured her, slipping his arm around her waist as they walked between the red brick buildings toward the apartment. Once inside he took her in his arms and again her misgivings faded away. "By the way," he whispered, "you look absolutely gorgeous in that dress. Will you wear it again soon?"

"But, Alex—" His mouth closed over hers before she could say any more, and she felt his hands slide along her back until he located the tab on the zipper. He was so warm and strong against her that, try as she might, Gretchen couldn't summon the strength to resist. Deep inside, she knew she didn't want to. She was falling in love with Alex Carson, in spite of her best efforts to the contrary, and that was complicating everything. Somehow she was going to have to work it all out, but that could wait till morning. She wrapped both arms around his neck and ran the tip of her tongue across his lips. She felt his body shiver before his open mouth was on hers.

"My bed or yours?" he whispered. His hands slipped inside her dress.

She ran her fingers down the front of his shirt and then around the inside of his suit jacket. "How about yours? It's closer."

He laughed and led her to his bedroom. He tossed his jacket and tie across the back of a chair. The room was dark except for the light from the moon, which bathed the bed in shimmering silver. As Alex pulled back the comforter and eased her down on the bed, Gretchen found his scent lingering on the pillow, that crisp, masculine scent she knew so well. She watched him remove his clothes, admiring his trim, powerful body, and as he came back to her, she wrapped her arms around him and held him close.

Alex slipped her dress off, and somehow her stockings disappeared, too, leaving her clad in nothing but a pair of red lace panties and a matching bra. "This is much sexier on you than on the drying rack," he murmured as he ran his finger along the edge of the bra.

Beneath the sheer lace Gretchen felt her breasts tingling when he caressed her. She expected him to finish undressing her, but Alex was in no hurry. He slid one of his legs across her hips, pinning her to the bed, and she felt him swelling against her. Waves of heat converged inside Gretchen. Surely now he'd take off all her clothes.

With agonizing slowness, he slipped one satin strap from her shoulder and kissed her bare skin, pressing her body tightly against him and forcing her to lie still.

"Alex, please—" She sucked in her breath as he slid the other strap off her shoulder, continuing to touch and tease her with his lips and his tongue. "Please, please," she begged him again. She tried to move, but he'd pinned her tightly against the sheets.

"What do you want?" he whispered hoarsely. "Tell me. Tell me, exactly." He eased his fingers inside the lace bra.

"Take it off, Alex," she gasped. "Please take it off."

"Like this?" He eased the fabric down a millimeter farther.

"No, all the way off," she moaned. She writhed beneath him and reached for the clasp of her bra.

He grabbed her hand. "I'm going to do that, Gretchen, but not yet," he said as he feathered kisses across her breasts. "Remember, we have all night." He caught the lace in his teeth, and she felt her bra inch down ever so slightly as he teased her with the tip of his tongue. When Gretchen thought she could stand it no longer, her breasts spilled free.

He touched and caressed her, which was what Gretchen had thought she wanted, but now it wasn't enough. "Alex, I can't stand this one more minute."

Reaching under the edge of her panties, he pressed his hand firmly against her. "You don't have to," he told her. "You don't have to wait."

"But Alex—" She couldn't say any more. His hand was moving, pressing. Heat converging like fire overwhelmed her. She closed her eyes and let the world swirl away. The she felt him inside her and her hips were free, rocking in his rhythm.

"Come with me, Gretchen," he urged her, and the feeling stirred again, building to an even greater intensity until finally he took her in a hard, driving explosion.

10

THE CANARY'S SHRILL SONG poured into the silence. Gretchen pulled the pillow over her head, but the sound cut right through. She sat bolt upright. That's when she realized she wasn't in her own bed.

"Damn!" Alex swore softly. "I forgot to cover the cage last night."

Gretchen rested her head on her knees. "Alex, that bird has to go."

"He's going, as soon as we can get him out of here," Alex promised. He pulled Gretchen down against him. "Good morning," he said, kissing her gently. Tweety trilled louder.

"That is absolutely the most obnoxious bird in existence," Gretchen declared, snuggling against Alex. "If it weren't for the stupid bird, we could have slept another hour." And then wakened slowly and been together in the gentle light of morning, she added silently.

"We could try ignoring him," Alex suggested.

"Fat chance." Sitting up again, Gretchen pulled the sheet around her.

Alex sat up beside her and leaned against her shoulder. "Then let's get dressed and take a ride out to McLean. We'll stop for breakfast on the way."

"With Tweety?"

"Oh, yeah, I forgot. Well, we'll eat breakfast here and then we'll go."

"Right." Gretchen hopped out of bed and scooped up her clothes. "Race you to the bathroom, Yuppie." After a quick shower, Gretchen put on a pair of jeans and a blue cotton sweater, then ate a bowl of cereal and read the paper while she waited for Alex. Despite her misgivings about going to his mother's house, she liked the idea of a ride on a gorgeous spring morning. She was even curious about the house—as long as she could see it without his mother.

With the cage cover on, Tweety was blessedly quiet as Alex drove along the George Washington Parkway then up a winding road lined with large, colonial houses. The grass and the trees were bathed in fragile spring green, punctuated by brilliant yellow daffodils and some early tulips bursting with red blossoms. As Gretchen looked out the window, each house seemed bigger than the last, many of them set on hills and along the edges of ravines. She was so caught up by it all that she was startled when Alex turned his Porsche into a wide circular drive.

He stopped the engine close to an imposing white house with tall pillars and thick azalea bushes across the front. Stately trees flanked the porch. The hills behind the house were laden with clusters of fragile dogwoods and still more azaleas in countless shades of pink.

"Your mother lives here all by herself?" Gretchen gazed up at the long row of windows on the second floor where the bedrooms must be.

"Since Dad died she's talked about selling and moving into something smaller, but I don't think she ever will," Alex said as he got out of the car. "She's lived here for too many years. She knows all the neighbors and she's close to the club. Those things are important to her now." Alex took Tweety's cage out of the back seat.

"Then this is where you grew up?" Gretchen asked as they walked toward the double oak doors at the front of the house.

"We moved here when I was in first grade, and I really don't remember living anywhere else. I'm sort of attached to the place, too," he added, unlocking the door.

The first thing that struck Gretchen when she stepped inside was the size of the foyer. It was almost as long as the trailer where she had lived in West Virginia. And the wall covering— Without even touching it she knew the muted floral design was silk. Alex laid his keys on a table beneath the gilt-edged mirror, and Gretchen followed him into the living room where her shoes sank deep into the plush carpeting. She watched as he hung the bird cage on its stand in front of a sunny bay window. As soon as the cover came off Tweety burst into song.

"Why don't you make yourself comfortable while I fill his water cup," Alex suggested.

Gretchen nodded, but after Alex left the room she couldn't quite bring herself to sit down on either of the light blue velvet wing chairs in front of the marble fireplace. Instead she eased around the sofa, done in pastel stripes no doubt to compliment the blue chairs, and went over to the baby grand piano. She had wanted to learn to play the piano as far back as she could remember. There had been an old upright in the Sunday school room, and sometimes when no one else was around she would press down one key at a time, trying to figure out how all the notes blended together to make music. She ran her fingers lightly over the mellow mahogany wood.

"Do you play?"

Gretchen quickly took her hand away from the piano when she heard Alex's voice. "Oh, no. Do you?"

Alex slid the water cup into Tweety's cage. "I had six years of lessons from Miss Pruneface—that's what I called her—and all I remember is this." He sat down on the bench, opened the lid and began to plunk out a raucous version of "Chopsticks." "Here, you do the right hand." He took Gretchen's fingers and placed them on the keys. "Okay, now." He began to beat the time with his head. The tempo moved faster and faster until the music was nothing more than a jumble of sounds and they both were laughing too hard to continue.

"There, in only one lesson you're as good as I am." Alex grinned and closed the piano.

She followed him into the dining room which was even more elegant than the living room. Hardwood floors gleamed around the edge of an Oriental rug in deep maroons and blues. A crystal chandelier hung over the Queen Anne style table, and the china cabinet was replete with silver pieces. Gretchen swallowed hard. "I can't imagine one person taking care of all of this. Just polishing that silver tea set would take hours."

"Mother's been lucky. The help is very reliable. She has an excellent gardener, and the cleaning lady has been with her for years."

The help. Gretchen winced. Her mother had been referred to as "the help." She'd actually heard the reference only once. It had been a Saturday afternoon when she'd gone to get her mother from a cleaning job because Nancy needed her. The woman who owned the house was angry because her mother couldn't stay. As they'd left, Gretchen had heard the woman tell a visiting friend: "It's so hard to find good help nowadays. You have to take what you can get." Soon afterward her mother had lost the cleaning job because she had missed too many days when Nancy was sick. Gretchen had never forgotten that woman and had never forgiven her.

Alex took Gretchen's hand. "Let's go upstairs and I'll show you my room."

She followed him silently up the staircase and down the hall to a room with two shelves of baseball trophies and an array of sports pennants covering one wall. All that space for one child, and still there a decade later as though he'd never left. To Gretchen, that was incomprehensible.

"Mother says she's keeping this room ready for visiting grandchildren." Alex chuckled. "It's one of those broad hints."

Gretchen shook her head.

"What's the matter, Gretchen?"

"It all seems so big, and there are so many things," she said.

Alex shrugged. "It's comfortable, but it's not really that big. Your house couldn't have been too much smaller with five of you."

Gretchen didn't answer. She wished she hadn't come with Alex. He knew virtually nothing of her background, and that was no accident. From the beginning, Gretchen had known the contrast between them was vivid, but seeing this house where he'd spent his childhood brought the picture into sharp focus. And now that she'd seen it, she would never be able to escape it. She remembered her mother telling her, "Don't be ashamed of where you came from. Everybody's the same inside." But she and Alex weren't the same, and they never would be. It wasn't just the money, it was the attitudes bred by money. The expectations. Alex was a thoroughbred, and she wasn't. Nothing would ever change that.

"Gretchen, something's wrong."

She looked up to see him staring at her and realized she'd been far away. "No, really, everything is fine." She attempted a smile. "Hadn't we better be going? I have to get ready for work."

He put his hands on her shoulders, then gently stroked her cheek. "I suppose we had better go. I have work this afternoon, too."

"I didn't know dentists worked on Saturdays."

"Depends on the dentist. Ed and I have some special people who come in on Saturdays. Most of them can't get there any other time."

Probably high-powered executives who couldn't find time in their schedules during the week. That was the kind of practice Alex would have, Gretchen decided.

"It's too bad we can't stay long enough for you to have a chance to meet my mother properly," Alex said.

"I don't think she's dying to meet me, Alex, after the last time—"

"She'd laugh about that now," he interjected. "We'll come back another time. There are some stables near here. Maybe we can go riding."

Gretchen turned away. She'd never been on a horse in her life, but that wasn't the problem. The problem was he was making too many plans. He was talking about a future that didn't exist. She felt his arm around her waist as they walked down the stairs.

"I want us to have a house like this some day, Gretchen, but farther out in the country. Maybe we can even have our own horses."

"Alex, stop!" Gretchen pulled away from him and bolted down the stairs.

By the time he caught up with her she was outside, leaning against the big oak tree in the front yard. "Gretchen, what happened?"

He looked puzzled and hurt, and she hated what she was about to do. "Nothing, Yuppie. It just got a little stifling in there."

"What's wrong with you, Gretchen? Whatever your problem is, it didn't start here. I felt it last night at the restaurant, but when we got home everything seemed all right. What the hell is the matter?"

She looked directly at him, her blue eyes flashing. "It's no good, Alex. I've come a long way and I've done it by myself but I'll never be on your level, no matter what I do."

Alex frowned. "I don't understand."

"You don't know anything about me, Alex. Didn't that ever strike you as odd?"

"Not particularly. You don't know much about me, either. I figured we both had pretty ordinary childhoods."

Gretchen's laugh was bitter. "It all depends on what you call ordinary. While you were taking piano lessons and dancing lessons and going to society parties, I was growing up in a trailer in West Virginia sharing a bed with my two sisters. Not a bedroom, Yuppie, a bed. We were never sure where the next meal was coming from. Without government food stamps we probably would have starved to death."

"So that's it." Alex shoved his hands in his pockets and stared at his feet.

"Not quite. My mother cleaned for women like your mother and she was poor till the day she died. She always blamed herself because she couldn't afford good enough medical care for Nancy. After Nancy died, she just gave up."

Alex's eyes sought Gretchen's, but he made no move to touch her. "And that's why Joyce decided to become a doctor and why you're working so hard to help her, isn't it?"

"Brilliant deduction, Yuppie. Now take me home or I'll be late to work." She stalked off toward the Porsche.

As he walked back to lock the house, Alex tried to figure out what to do next. He didn't give a damn about Gretchen's background. He liked her just the way she was. But he'd never convince her of that. He slammed the front door hard. Money was just a way of making yourself comfortable and guaranteeing some control over your life. He'd never convince Gretchen of that, either, but on the way home he decided to try.

"I don't know why you're so damned belligerent about my background," he observed as they turned onto the parkway. "You've done all right. You're a teacher. You're living in a nice apartment. You like nice things...like that new red dress you bought. That came out of one of the top fashion houses, and it looks it." He glanced at her, but she was staring out the window, her head turned so he could barely see her face. Since she appeared to at least be listening to him, he decided to go on. "There's nothing wrong with having money, Gretchen, and being able to buy the things you want. What if you were to win the lottery? Then you would have a whole lot of money. How would you reconcile that?"

For the first time since they'd left his mother's house, Gretchen looked at him. "That was an unfair, low blow, and you know it."

Alex smiled. He'd finally gotten through. "Well, how would you?"

"Winning the lottery is a whole different thing," she continued heatedly. "It's like having lightning strike."

"But then you'd have more money than I do, Gretchen. Would that change how you felt about me?"

She stared straight ahead. That was an unfair question and just showed how far apart they really were.

"Answer me, Gretchen," Alex demanded. "Would that solve it for you?"

"We'll never know, will we, unless I buy my lottery ticket," she shot back. "Pull over there. I'm running late."

Alex sighed. She was the most damned stubborn woman he'd ever met. But maybe he'd given her something to think about. While Gretchen waited in line to buy her lottery ticket, Alex picked up a loaf of rye bread and a carton of two percent milk.

"I suppose you've never bought a lottery ticket in your life," she challenged when he joined her in line.

"Nope."

"That figures. You already have it all so you don't need to play the lottery."

He reached into his back pocket. "As a matter of fact, maybe I will buy a ticket," he said. "How do you do it?"

"Pick a number, Yuppie. Pick your lucky number." Gretchen laughed, but her laughter was forced. She didn't want Alex to play the lottery. To him it was nothing but a joke, and he was being almost patronizing by buying a ticket. Then Gretchen had an even more unsettling thought. What if he won? He wouldn't. The odds against it were overwhelming. But what if he did? Gretchen pushed away the fear as irrational. She had a better chance than he did. After all, she played every week, and he'd never bought a ticket before.

"I've got my number," he said with a smug expression as he pulled the money out of his wallet. "A sure winner."

"Yeah, I'll bet. Let's see, you picked your birthday or your license number or your mother's phone number—"

"None of the above." Alex smiled at her. "I chose the date I moved in with you."

"No way, Yuppie. That's not going to win anything." Gretchen didn't add that she ought to know. She'd picked that number three weeks running.

AFTER ALEX FINISHED at the office late that afternoon, he went to take one last look at his condominium before signing the final papers. He surveyed the empty living room with mixed feelings. Everything was exactly as he had envisioned, with one exception. Gretchen wasn't part of it. He wasn't quite sure just how, or when, he had woven her into the condominium dream, but somehow, at some time, he had. When he first bought the place he had intended to turn it into the ultimate bachelor pad, but now he thought differently, possibly because he no longer felt like the ultimate bachelor. For the first time, he understood why. He had fallen in love with Gretchen and he wanted her to live with him in the condominium and be part of his life.

He knelt and ran his hand over the smooth tile hearth in front of the fireplace, imagining the warmth of a blazing fire on a cold, snowy evening. He and Gretchen would be lying together in a nest of throw pillows, sharing quiet moments and a bottle of wine. They would probably make love, either in front of the fire or in the master bedroom suite. He had already decided that a king-size bed would be the first piece of furniture he bought. A king-size bed covered with a down-filled comforter.

He wandered into the kitchen and opened several cabinets, savoring their fresh, pungent wood aroma. The deep cabinet above the built-in oven would hold Gretchen's giant-sized box of cereal. And his ten-pound bag of Chinese rice would fit right next to her cereal. Funny how things like that worked out. After a while all the various items that belonged to each of them individually just blended together. He closed the cabinets, poked his head into the refrigerator and pulled out the meat drawer, envisioning her one-pound package of sliced bologna in there.

Shaking his head with amazement that he could ever have fallen for a woman like Gretchen, he headed into the bedroom. The brilliant afternoon sun streamed through the floor-to-ceiling windows that faced west and ran the length of the room. No early morning sunrises here to wake them up. Only glorious sunsets and a spectacular view of the Potomac River. This bedroom was made for them.

And so was the bathroom. Alex grinned as he turned the water on and off in each of the two vanity sinks, then opened and closed both sides of the double medicine cabinet. Some things were better not shared. Then again, some things, like the shower and the whirlpool tub, were nicer with company. Maybe he'd pick up a bar of that rose-scented soap Gretchen used and have it waiting in the tub.

Satisfied that the place was as promised, Alex rode the elevator down to the building office to sign the papers. Finally he owned something. Granted, the condominium was a modest beginning, but it was all his. He had a home to start out in, a place for dreams to begin. Now he could ask Gretchen to marry him.

Marriage? Alex was startled by the sudden thought, and he mulled it over as he walked down the street to his Porsche. The longer he thought about it, the better the idea seemed. Gradually he realized it had been growing for weeks, maybe even months, since that first morning in the kitchen when she'd appeared in her T-shirt. From that moment on he had been consumed by her. And somehow he knew that situation wouldn't change for the rest of his life. He really had no choice except to marry her.

Having made his decision, Alex determined he wanted to marry Gretchen as soon as possible, which meant he needed to ask her as soon as possible. As he started the car he berated himself for not talking to her sooner, before that disastrous visit to his mother's house. Well, she'd get over that. The differences in how they had grown up were insignificant. What really counted was now, and how much he loved her. All he had to do was convince Gretchen.

GRETCHEN SAT ON THE COUCH with her arms wrapped around her knees, staring at the aquarium. Almost a week since she'd seen Alex. The angelfish swam by, and Gretchen could almost swear it glared at her, which was perfectly ridiculous. Fish didn't glare, but if they did, Alex was the one the fish should be glaring at. What a mess. And it was all Alex the Yuppie's fault. If he hadn't moved into her apartment, she wouldn't know him. And if she didn't know him, she couldn't have fallen in love with him.

She watched as the angelfish blew a column of bubbles and glided behind some sea grass. That stupid fish sure led an easy life. All he had to do was swim around and munch on a few tasty brine shrimp now and then. He didn't have to worry about being in love with the wrong person.

"Open up! I know you're in there!" The coarse voice penetrated the front door as though it weren't there. Lew! Gretchen froze. She'd almost forgotten. But he hadn't. He wanted his money. She sat perfectly still and didn't make a sound.

"Lady, you're asking for trouble."

Don't you threaten me, Gretchen thought. But she didn't say it. There was no way he could be absolutely sure she was home unless she answered him.

"You've gotta come out some time," he said, "and before you do, you better cough up the payment or Lew's going to give you a little help."

After several moments of silence, she heard his heavy footsteps on the stairs. Once the sound had faded, Gretchen grabbed her purse and dumped it on the couch. She felt like a prisoner, afraid to go out because she might run into Lew, afraid to answer the phone because he'd be on the other end. She wondered what he'd meant about her coming up with the payment or him giving her a little help. Whatever he had in mind, she didn't think she liked it.

She counted her money, every penny of it, and then she counted it again, just in case she'd missed something. There wasn't enough, and there wasn't going to be any time soon. She hadn't expected to have some of her performances canceled without pay. And she hadn't expected Shenanigans to hire another performer because they thought she was stretched too thin.

The phone rang, and Gretchen didn't move. It was probably Lew. He phoned all the time, too. By the fourth ring, she stood up. She had to answer in case the call was about a job. She picked up the receiver and sighed with relief when she heard Trudy's voice.

"I heard that man at your door," Trudy said, dispensing with the preliminaries. "Are you all right?"

"Yes, I'm fine. When the phone rang, I was afraid it was him again."

"This doesn't sound good," Trudy said. "I'll be right over."

When Trudy walked in, Gretchen might have hugged her if Trudy hadn't been carrying her ever-present mug of coffee. What she needed was a friend and some quick answers.

"So why's that loan shark bugging you?" Trudy demanded. "I almost went out there and told him a thing or two."

"I've got a real problem," Gretchen admitted. She sat down on the couch and gathered up the contents of her purse while Trudy went into the kitchen to get her ashtray.

"Talk," Trudy said. "We'll figure something out."

"I missed another loan payment yesterday. I simply don't have the money, and there's no way I'm going to get it, either."

"You're right. You have got a problem." Trudy lit a cigarette. "I've still got a hundred and twenty-five of my two hundred dollars left, if that will help."

"I am not going to take your money," Gretchen said firmly. "But even added to my sixty-nine dollars and twenty-seven cents, that wouldn't be enough, anyway. Everything would have worked out just fine if those jobs hadn't been canceled."

"Have you told Alex about this?"

"No," Gretchen answered sharply. "I don't want to discuss it with Alex. Besides, he's never here anyway."

Trudy took a drag of her cigarette and looked thoughtfully at Gretchen. "That's funny. With you not working so much, I'd have expected you two would be seeing more of each other."

"Well, we haven't. He hasn't been home one night this week."

"Wonder what he's up to."

"I have no idea," Gretchen answered icily. "I haven't seen him since Saturday when we took that stupid bird back to his mother's."

"From the sound of things, Saturday wasn't such a good experience, either."

"That's one way to put it." Gretchen stood up and walked restlessly across the living room. "You should see where he grew up. It's a mansion in an area with a whole lot of others just like it. I'm not in that league, Trudy, and I never will be."

"Get off it, Gretchen." Trudy mashed out her cigarette and picked up her coffee. "You're all hung up with being this poverty-stricken kid riddled with insecurities because other people had more than you. Grow up. Be who you are now."

Gretchen curled up on the couch and stared at Trudy. "That's really easy for you to say. And, by the way, I wish you'd never bought that red silk dress at the thrift shop."

"Why not? You were a knockout in that dress. Don't tell me he didn't like it!"

"Oh, he liked it all right," Gretchen answered. "He also recognized the designer label, and he keeps talking about my expensive tastes and my spending all that money."

Trudy shook her head. "So why didn't you just come out and tell him where it came from?"

"Be serious."

"I'm being very serious. Does Alex know anything about your background?"

"I told him Saturday."

"And what did he say?"

Gretchen thought for a moment. Exactly what had he said? He hadn't sounded shocked, or even sympathetic. "He asked if I won the lottery if it would make any difference."

"Would it?" Trudy asked.

"It might. I honestly don't know."

"Then you'd better think through your feelings really carefully," Trudy advised, "because winning the lottery wouldn't make you or Alex any different people from what you already are."

"I suppose not, but it sure would make life easier."

"Speaking of life," Trudy said, lighting another cigarette, "you're going to have to do something about this loan payment. That man makes me nervous."

Gretchen shivered when she thought about Lew.

"Another car wash is probably out, at least right away," Trudy continued. "The owner of the gas station said the traffic jam cut into business. But I can ask. Maybe we'll get lucky."

"If I had anything valuable, I'd sell it, but all I've got is the car," Gretchen said.

"And how are you going to manage without a car? Remember how grim it was the week it was broken?" Trudy took a swallow of her coffee. "You know, it looks to me like Alex is your only option. I know you hate to ask him for money, but you've got to get that loan shark off your back."

"I can't ask Alex! He'll think I blew the money for the loan payment on the red dress."

"You *can* ask Alex. If he's got as much money as you say he has, he won't miss a few hundred dollars for awhile."

Gretchen shook her head determinedly. "No, I won't ask him."

"All right, suit yourself, but I'm out of suggestions."

After Trudy left, Gretchen paced for an hour trying to find another solution. She answered the phone, and this time it was Lew. First she listened, then she tried to reason with him, then, her hand trembling, she hung up. Once she had a dial tone, she laid the receiver on the table. No matter what other calls she missed, she couldn't deal with Lew again. Restless and unhappy, she got ready for bed and finally, the last thing before she turned out the light, she walked into the bathroom and scrawled a note to Alex.

Alex—
I missed a payment. Can you loan me $300.00? I'll start paying you back as soon as I can.
                                                    Gretchen

When Alex arrived home near midnight, he walked into the bathroom and found Gretchen's note. He stared at it for a long time, realizing how hard it must have been for her to write those words. He started to make out a check for three hundred dollars, then tore it up. He'd get her cash and bring it home the next day at lunchtime. Maybe they would have some time to talk, too. He'd been so busy with his new condominium that he hadn't had a free night for the past week. But now everything was ready. The kitchen was stocked with groceries, including cereal and bologna, wood for the fireplace was stacked on the balcony and the king-sized bed had been delivered. On Saturday he'd take Gretchen to see the condominium and then he'd ask her to marry him.

After he washed and brushed his teeth, he wrote an answer to her note.

Dear Gretchen,
I'll be glad to loan you the money if you'll spend some time with me on Saturday. We'll worry about repayment later.
                                                         A.

When Alex arrived at the apartment the next day with three crisp hundred-dollar bills in his wallet, Gretchen was nowhere to be found, but she'd left a note on the mirror.

Whatever you say for Saturday. Under the circumstances, I guess you call the shots, Yuppie.

He pulled the piece of paper off the mirror and crumpled it in his hand. Damn, he hadn't meant to make her angry. Sometimes it wasn't easy to arrange a surprise. He dropped the hundred-dollar bills on the counter by the sink, weighted them down with the edge of the Water Pik and wrote himself a reminder: "Buy champagne." He hoped his plan worked. Gretchen could really be stubborn sometimes.

11

SATURDAY. The day Gretchen had been dreading. First she had to face Alex after borrowing the money. Then she had to go wherever he had in mind—after all, under the circumstances, how could she refuse? And what if he wanted to do something awful like go to his mother's? She heard the food processor whirring away and she knew he was up. Might as well get it over with. Barefooted, she walked into the kitchen and headed directly for the coffeepot.

From behind the sports section, Alex watched her reach into the cabinet for her cereal. Knowing what she wore under that T-shirt didn't make it any less seductive. He'd like to take her right back to bed. Maybe that's exactly what he'd do when they got to the condominium, after he'd asked her to marry him.

"Good morning," he said cheerfully as she brought her coffee and cereal to the table.

Gretchen set down her breakfast. "Alex, why do you have to run the food processor every Saturday morning?"

"Because that's how I make my yogurt shake. And you'll notice I never do it before ten o'clock, just for you."

Gretchen grimaced. They'd had this discussion before, and she never won. Besides, there were other things she had to talk to him about. She really wanted to ask where he'd been all week. But she didn't. Instead she swallowed hard and did what she had to do.

"I guess I should thank you for loaning me the money." The words made her cereal taste like cardboard, but they had to be said. "You realize I have no idea when I can pay any of it back," she added.

"No hurry," Alex answered. "Maybe we'll call it my contribution to Joyce's education."

"Thanks, but no thanks, Yuppie," Gretchen retorted. "It was a loan. I'll pay it back."

"Don't be so defensive, Gretchen." Alex laid down the paper. "It's just money."

They'd had that discussion before, too, and Gretchen didn't want to have it again. She changed the subject. "By the way, exactly what do you have in mind for today?" she asked him warily. "If it's something like going to your mother's—"

"No chance," Alex interrupted. "I have a surprise for you, but you have to wait till you get there to find out what it is."

"A surprise?" Gretchen suddenly felt like the sun had come out. Ever since she'd found his note, she'd been sure he was planning to drag her back to McLean. Maybe the day wasn't going to be so grim after all.

"But you're never going to find out what it is unless you hurry up and get dressed," he complained.

"All right. Just let me check the lottery numbers." She rifled through the pile of newspaper on the chair until she found the right section. "It'll only take a minute."

Alex shook his head and went back to reading the baseball scores. She didn't give up. Too bad she couldn't actually win the lottery. That would solve a lot of problems.

Scanning the page quickly, Gretchen checked the number. As she started to close the paper, she felt something akin to a huge ice chunk form in her stomach. She read the number again, very slowly. It wasn't her number, but it was only one digit off from the number she'd picked the three weeks before. The number Alex had picked. Could he have come that close? Or worse yet....

"Alex, what lottery number did you pick?" She tried to ask casually, but her voice sounded strange, even to her.

Alex looked at her over the paper. "I told you. I picked the date I moved in with you. Why?"

"I know that," Gretchen said impatiently, "but you had to add numbers to it to make it work because there aren't enough digits. What is the actual number on your ticket?"

Alex thought hard. "Two . . . twelve . . . I don't remember. It's on my dresser."

"Well, go get it."

Alex chuckled as he got up. "I suppose you're going to tell me I won the lottery."

"Just go get the ticket," Gretchen demanded. Not that she really thought he'd won. But he'd come close, at least as close as she had that one time she'd thought for a split second her dream had come true. And that wasn't fair, not on his first try.

"Here you go," Alex said, returning to the kitchen with the ticket in his hand. "For a minute there, I couldn't find the ticket. Not that it would have mattered, but you'd have always wondered."

Gretchen wasn't paying any attention. She was holding the ticket just below the printed number in the paper and matching the digits one by one, again and again and again. She felt the color drain from her face as she laid the ticket on the table. "Alex," she said in a hollow voice, "you just won three million dollars."

He snatched the newspaper out of her hands. "Let me see that." Holding the ticket below the printed number just as she had, he stared at the identical rows of numbers. Slowly he raised his eyes to hers and broke into an enormous grin. "By God, I did." Then the realization hit him.

"I won, Gretchen! I won!" he shouted. "I won the lottery." He picked her up off the chair and swung her around and clamped her into a huge bear hug. "I won! I actually won," he said incredulously. He held her away from him. "Do you realize what that means?"

"Congratulations, Alex," Gretchen said automatically. "I'm very happy for you."

"Three million dollars." He spun away from her, waving the ticket over his head. "I can't believe it."

Jerking open the refrigerator, he pulled out a half-full bottle of red wine and took two glasses from the cupboard. "We'll have a toast," he proclaimed, "to instant millions. And then we're going to celebrate. You name it, we'll do it. Anything, absolutely anything."

Gretchen watched him silently, trying to quell the anger and disappointment that surged through her. She knew she should be happy for him. After all, he'd just won three million dollars. A fortune. But all she could think of was that it was so damned unfair. Why hadn't she won? That would have been her three million dollars. She was the one who played the lottery faithfully every week. She was the one who needed the money so desperately. The rich get richer and the poor get poorer . . . the refrain played over and over in her head. He'd had everything he wanted to begin with, and now he had more.

"What are you going to do with all that money, Alex?" she asked. It hurt to even ask him the question.

"How the hell should I know? I haven't even picked it up yet. But, I promise you, we'll think of something. Our worries are over, Gretchen. Don't you realize what it means? Aren't you excited?"

"Of course. I told you I'm very happy for you, Alex." What did he mean about our worries being over? It was his money. He was the one who had won the lottery. She still had all the same money problems she had always had.

"Maybe we should take a trip," he suggested, turning a chair around and sitting down with his elbows resting on the chair back. "Where would you like to go? Anywhere in the world, just name it."

Gretchen stared at her wineglass. She remembered him asking her if she won the lottery whether it would make any difference in how she felt about him. The question he hadn't asked was what if *he* won. Now she knew. The gap between them, which had seemed almost impossible to bridge before, was now even wider. So wide she couldn't even comprehend it.

"Come on," he prodded. "Make a choice. Africa, Australia, maybe a South Sea island.... The world is ours, Gretchen."

Slowly she met his eyes. "Wrong, Yuppie. The world is yours. Take your money and go enjoy it." She watched his excitement fade and a bewildered expression take its place.

"What's the matter, Gretchen?"

"You mean you haven't figured it out?"

"No, I haven't." He stood up and paced across the kitchen where he leaned against the counter and looked at her, still appearing puzzled.

"Then let me spell it out for you. I'm flat broke. Every week I hope against hope that maybe my dream will come true and I'll win the lottery. You buy one ticket. You don't even bother to check the number. And what happens? You win and I lose. Again. That's damned unfair, Alex. You didn't even need the money."

Alex's expression hardened. "So you're mad because I won the lottery and you didn't?"

"That sounds like the way you'd explain it. You can't even see the ultimate injustice."

"Bullshit!" Alex exploded. "What I see is someone so blinded by her own petty problems that she doesn't get the big picture. You're so busy feeling sorry for yourself that you don't have time for anyone or anything else."

Gretchen sprang to her feet. "You're a mean, ignorant, conceited . . . *dentist*."

"Thanks, I'll remember that."

"And furthermore you can get out of my apartment. I wouldn't want you to spend one more minute of your life slumming." Gretchen gripped the back of the chair so hard her knuckles turned white. "After all, you're really rich now. You can live any place you want."

"Gretchen—" His tone softened and he took a step toward her.

"Get out, Yuppie," she shouted, backing away. "Get out of my life."

Alex stood still for a long moment, his muscles taut. "All right, Gretchen," he answered in a voice that was calm, "if that's how you feel, I'll do exactly that."

He walked out of the kitchen and moments later Gretchen heard the front door of the apartment slam hard. She grabbed her wineglass off the table and smashed it into the sink, where it shattered into a million pieces. "Take that you . . . you . . . Yuppie," she shouted into the silence. "That's what I think of your three million dollars. I hope I never see you again. Ever!"

GRETCHEN SPENT most of the day in a blind rage. By the time she got home that night, she still hadn't forgiven Alex for winning her three million dollars. However, she was beginning to regret some of the things she'd said to him.

"Alex?" she called as she walked inside the apartment. He didn't answer. "Alex?" she called again. Her voice echoed in the silence. He must be out celebrating, she decided. She felt a small pang of regret when she realized she could be with him.

Then she flipped on the light and noticed his bike was gone. That was odd. He didn't usually ride at night. He said it wasn't safe, even with a light. Gretchen looked around. The apartment was so quiet, and something about the living room was different. When her gaze swept the bookcase, she knew what it was.

The aquarium was gone. The pump no longer hummed steadily, spewing streams of bubbles into the lighted tank. Uneasily, Gretchen walked into the bathroom. Her bath powder sat alone on the counter beside the sink. No Water Pik, no baking soda, no hydrogen peroxide. "My God," she whispered, and rushed toward Alex's room. She stopped in the doorway. Except for the bed and the dresser, everything was gone—the bookcase, the curtains, the assortment of junk on the dresser top. Alex had moved out.

Gretchen walked slowly across the room to pick up a piece of paper partially hidden by one of the legs of the dresser. It was a receipt of some sort. She studied it in the shaft of light from the hall. *One long-stemmed rose, $6.95*, it read. Severely shaken, she wandered to the living room. That must have been the rose Alex left for her the day they went out to dinner. She stared at the receipt, realizing it was the only tangible evidence she had left that Alex Carson even existed.

Sinking down onto the moss-green chair, Gretchen spent more than an hour staring at the empty spot where the fish tank had been. She was almost used to those fish, especially the blue one with the big fins. She couldn't get over how quiet everything seemed. After awhile she turned on the television and was relieved when its electronic voices filled up the silence.

She was ready for bed and passing through the kitchen to get a glass of milk when she found the note Alex had left on the kitchen table. Unlike all the other notes, it was written in ink on a piece of white typing paper. He'd laid his door key on top of it. Gretchen picked up the key, holding it tight in her hand as she read.

Dear Gretchen,
Paid the rent for the next three months. Arrangements made to settle your pawnshop account as thanks for your help with the lottery.

Sincerely,
Alex

Gretchen wadded the note into a tight ball and threw it across the kitchen. She felt neither grateful nor angry at what she'd read. She simply felt totally and completely alone. Alex had carefully fulfilled all his obligations. He had taken pains to be generous and fair. And he had made it quite clear that he wasn't coming back.

"Dammit, I don't care." She walked purposefully into the bedroom, turned off the light and burrowed down under the covers. But she didn't sleep because, in the intimacy of night, she couldn't lie to herself. She did care. She cared a great deal. However insurmountable their problems, she'd fallen in love with Alex Carson. Then she'd essentially thrown him out and slammed the door. "How can you be so dumb?" she whispered to herself. The answer eluded her as the clock ticked away the early morning hours.

As far as Alex was concerned, the weekend was the worst he'd ever spent. He didn't give a damn about winning the lottery. In fact, he hadn't even claimed the money.

And his new condominium was a bust. None of what he'd brought from Gretchen's apartment was unpacked. Cardboard cartons, sports equipment, kitchen appliances and clothes were strewn from one end of the place to the other. His aquarium sat empty on the fireplace hearth, and the angelfish swam mournfully in the two-pound peanut-butter jar he'd used to transport it.

In addition to everything else, his back ached from sleeping on the lumpy sofa, which had been delivered from storage along with the rest of his furniture. He could have slept in the new king-size bed, but he wanted no part of it without Gretchen. He had never been so damned mad at a woman in his life. And he had never missed one so acutely. The last thing he did before he left for work on Monday morning was pitch the bologna in the trash on top of the giant-size box of cereal.

"Morning, Ed," he muttered as he hung his bicycle helmet on the coatrack in the reception room of his office.

"From the looks of you, moving into that new condominium of yours really did you in." Ed plugged in the coffee maker.

"Yeah, I guess so."

"Getting settled can be a real bitch," Ed said sympathetically. "But having a woman around will help. Gretchen can get the kitchen organized and pick out the drapes and in no time you'll feel right at home."

Alex pulled on his clinic jacket. Ed's scenario was exactly what he'd had in mind before everything fell apart. "Gretchen isn't living in the condominium with me," he stated flatly.

Ed's eyebrows raised up over the rims of his glasses. "She isn't?"

"Nope. Is that coffee ready yet?"

"Not quite."

Alex opened the appointment book and ran his finger down the day's list. He knew Ed was waiting for him to elaborate, but he was so mad he didn't want to talk about it.

"I suppose it's none of my business," Ed began.

Alex had figured he'd ask. In fact he'd known the question would begin just that way.

"What happened between you two?" Ed continued. "I was under the impression you were ready to pop the big question."

"I was," Alex answered, thinking about the champagne in the back of his refrigerator. As soon as he got back to the condominium tonight, he'd throw that in the trash, too. Imported from France or not.

"And?" Ed prompted.

"And I won the lottery and now Gretchen won't have anything to do with me. Isn't the coffee ready yet?"

"Say that again?" Ed sank into the receptionist's chair.

"Isn't that damned coffee ready?"

Ed stared at him. "You're telling me that you, Alex Carson, D.D.S., my partner for the last four years, have won three million dollars in the Virginia State Lottery? My God, man, that's a fortune."

"Yes," Alex agreed, "that's a fortune." Drops of coffee sizzled on the warming plate as he pulled out the pot and filled his mug.

"And then you're telling me that's the reason your girlfriend dumped you? Is that what I heard you say?"

"Yep."

"And that's all you can say—yep?"

Alex didn't answer. He knew how ludicrous the situation must seem to Ed. And it was ludicrous, but that didn't change the fact that being without Gretchen had left a huge hole in his life that all the money in the world couldn't fill.

"I'd say you both need to have your heads examined," Ed observed. He took off his glasses, held them up to the light, then began cleaning them. "Whatever happened to women wanting to marry men with money?"

"I told you before. Gretchen is weird about money." Alex took a long swallow of his coffee.

"There's weird and there's weird." Ed put his glasses on and stared at Alex. "Get your nose out of the appointment book, dammit, and look at me."

Grudgingly Alex complied.

"Now what gives you the idea this chick's as important as three million dollars?" Ed demanded. "Maybe you're better off without her."

Alex didn't answer. Maybe he was, but he certainly didn't feel better off.

"I can see you don't buy that," Ed commented.

"It's all so damned stupid!" Alex exploded. "If she'd just listen to reason—"

Alex stopped midsentence when the front door opened as the receptionist arrived for work.

"I take it this windfall isn't public knowledge?" Ed inquired.

"No!" Alex retorted. "It certainly isn't."

Ed stood up and walked away from the reception desk shaking his head.

ALEX RAN BEHIND SCHEDULE all day and was nearly an hour late finishing up his last patient. He assumed he was alone as he walked out of the examining room to pick up his bike helmet and ride home. But Ed was waiting for him.

"I see you made it through the day—finally," Ed noted.

"What are you still doing here?" Alex didn't want to talk to Ed or anyone else.

"Seems we didn't quite get our discussion finished this morning. I'll have to admit I've been thinking about it all day and judging from how long it took for you to finish up, I assume you have, too."

Alex sank down on the bench by the coatrack and rested his head in his hands. "I don't know what I'm going to do," he admitted.

"Do you love her?"

Alex slammed his fist down on the bench. "What kind of a question is that?"

"The same one your father would have asked you if he were here to do it. Do you love her?"

Alex scowled. "Yeah, dammit. I love her. I know she's a little flaky and I wish she could come to grips with this money thing, but I do love her. That's the whole problem."

"In that case, there's no point in trying to reason with you. Let's try a different angle. What are you going to do with this three million dollars that she's so burned up about you winning?"

"What do you mean?"

Ed paced around the reception desk then finally sat down. "Are you going to buy a yacht, breed race horses, open a safari resort in Africa— What do you have in mind?"

Alex was startled. He hadn't really seriously considered what he would do with his lottery winnings. He was pretty satisfied with his life as it was. He liked being a dentist, and he had a good income, which was going to be even better when he took over the whole practice after Ed retired.

"Three million dollars, Alex. Think about it," Ed pushed him.

Alex frowned. He was thinking about it. He already had the money he inherited from his father carefully invested to provide a nice cushion of security. He owned a condominium, and in a few years, when he was married and ready to have some kids, he'd buy a house, and probably one of those big vans. His Porsche wasn't exactly the thing to transport a growing family. And maybe he'd like to have a summer cottage on the North Carolina coastline, or take a trip once in a while. Other than that, he really had no burning desire to change his life-style.

"You know, Ed, odd as it sounds, I really don't know what to do with the three million. I'm already pretty well set financially. Maybe I could just not claim the money at all."

"That is the most asinine idea you've had yet," Ed told him bluntly.

"Why?" Alex thought it sounded pretty good.

"Because that's a cop-out and it won't solve anything. Take the money and do something constructive with it if you don't want to keep it for yourself. Maybe you can figure out something that is important to both you and Gretchen."

Alex stood up and paced across the reception room. Ed was probably right. He couldn't just walk away from three million dollars. That wouldn't get Gretchen back, anyway. It would just reinforce what she already thought of him. He remembered what his father had always told him about money: the point wasn't how much money you had, but what you did with it. Alex looked thoughtfully at Ed. "Maybe you've got something there. I could give it to a charity."

Ed laughed. "With that much money you could *be* a charity. Pick a group—the homeless, the hungry, old people, kids . . . you name it."

Kids. Alex rolled the idea around in his head. He and Gretchen did both care about kids. That was one reason she was a teacher, and he ran the free clinic on Saturdays. And they'd both gravitated to Susan immediately. Kids. Sick kids. Kids who needed special help. "Ed," he said, pacing briskly toward where his partner was sitting, "for an old guy about to retire, you come up with some pretty good ideas once in a while."

ON SATURDAY MORNING, after a terrible week, Gretchen woke up dreaming about the food processor. Several moments passed before she realized the sound she'd heard was someone pounding on her door. Alex. The thought propelled her out of bed. Alex had come back. Throwing on her robe, she raced to the hallway. She heard someone calling her name and grabbed the doorknob, shoving the dead bolt open at the same time. But when she opened the door, her spirits crashed.

"Trudy!" she exclaimed, her voice laden with disappointment.

In her nurse's uniform and obviously on her way to the hospital, Trudy marched in carrying the morning paper. "Have you seen it? Have you seen this?" she demanded waving the newspaper at Gretchen.

"No," Gretchen answered. "I just got up."

"That turkey who won the lottery last week still hasn't bothered to pick up his money," she announced indignantly. "It says so right here!" She thrust the paper at Gretchen, pointing to a small article on an inside page. "And do you know what else? Whoever won bought the ticket right over at Grisner's Drug Store!"

Gretchen skimmed the article, realizing she hadn't seen Trudy for a week, not since Alex left. Trudy didn't know . . . she'd have no way of knowing.

"Do you think there's a chance that the person who won has lost his ticket?" Trudy said hopefully. "Maybe it went through the laundry or something."

Gretchen shook her head. "No chance."

"Don't be such a pessimist. You don't know," Trudy chided.

"Oh yes, I do," Gretchen retorted. "Alex Carson won the lottery, and he's got the ticket in his pocket."

Trudy's mouth dropped open. "Alex won? You're kidding."

"Nope. I'm dead serious."

"But Alex doesn't even play the lottery," Trudy protested. "How could he win?"

"He bought one ticket," Gretchen said bitterly. "Because I dared him to. He used almost the exact number I played for three weeks. And he won."

"I can't believe it." Trudy sounded as if she was in shock. "I never thought I'd actually know somebody who won. Do you realize you're living with a millionaire—a genuine, bona fide millionaire?"

"Wrong again," Gretchen said.

"What do you mean, wrong again?" Trudy demanded.

"Just what I said. Wrong. Alex moved out."

With a stricken expression on her face, Trudy stared at Gretchen. "You mean for good?"

Gretchen nodded. The words made it sound so final.

"Oh, my God! What happened?"

"It's kind of a long story," Gretchen said. "Come on in the kitchen and I'll make some coffee. Some instant coffee," she added as Trudy followed her to the kitchen.

"Instant?" Trudy wrinkled her nose in distaste.

"Yep. Alex took his coffee maker." Gretchen filled a teakettle with water and set it on the stove. "And his microwave and his food processor." Gretchen remembered her disdain when Alex had first moved in with all his Yuppie appliances and realized she didn't feel that way any more. She watched the gas flames lick around the bottom of the still cold teakettle. So much had changed since Alex came, and none of it would ever go back the same way it was. Since he'd left, she had spent the most miserable week of her life, far worse than when the rent was overdue or she had missed a loan payment and Lew was banging on her door demanding money. She'd thought if those problems were ever solved, life would be wonderful. But it wasn't, and she didn't see how it was going to get any better.

"So what happened between you two?" Trudy asked again. "Everything seemed so good." When Gretchen still didn't answer, Trudy frowned and began stirring her coffee. "Wait a minute. How long has Alex been gone?"

"A week. Exactly a week today."

"That louse!" Trudy exploded. "That dirty bum. He lives here till he wins that money, and then he dumps you and takes off. If that isn't the lowest, meanest, most—"

"Hold it, Trudy," Gretchen interrupted. "That's not the way it happened." She struggled with the words. Now that her anger was gone, she felt so stupid and so sorry about what she'd done that she could barely talk about it. Finally she said it straight out. "I dumped him. When he won, I went off the deep end and ordered him to leave and said I never wanted to see him again."

Trudy stared at her incredulously. "Why did you do a dumb thing like that?"

"I don't know." Gretchen paced restlessly across the kitchen. "All week I've asked myself and I still don't know." She sank down on the chair across from Trudy. "I guess all my life, I've never had anything, and he's had it all, and then he won the lottery, too. It was so unfair that I blew up."

"And you argued and then what?"

"When I came home from work that night, he'd moved out. He left me a note saying he'd paid three months rent and he'd taken care of the loan from the pawnshop. I haven't heard from him since."

"Oh, my God," Trudy said again. "He even paid off the loan shark?"

Gretchen nodded.

Trudy shook her head in disbelief. "I've known people who've messed up their lives, but frankly, Gretchen, you win the prize."

"Thanks," Gretchen said. "That's just what I needed to hear."

"You're right," Trudy told her without sympathy. "You did. I'll come back after work and we'll see what we can figure out." She stood up and picked up her purse. "Actually, I'm filling in on pediatrics today so I'll see you when you come do your Clara routine."

"Not today," Gretchen said, as she walked Trudy to the door.

"Why not? The children count on you!"

"I just can't make myself do it, Trudy. Nobody needs a miserable clown."

After Trudy left, Gretchen took a shower and ate breakfast. She opened the newspaper and automatically turned to the winning lottery number for the week before she realized she didn't care. She hadn't bothered to buy a ticket. Pacing aimlessly through the apartment, she tried to decide what to do with her day. She didn't want to stay home, but she didn't want to go out, either. She didn't want to do anything. When the phone rang, she almost didn't answer it but then decided it was probably a job and as long as she wasn't going to be Clara, she might as well go.

"Gretchen, you have to come to the hospital," Trudy's voice announced as soon as Gretchen answered. "Susan is in surgery and her grandfather is here all alone."

"Oh, Trudy, I can't—" The only time she'd ever gone to the hospital without being Clara was that one day Alex took her. She couldn't go alone, not under these circumstances.

"You have to," Trudy said flatly.

"But, Trudy, I don't even know Susan's grandfather. And even if I did—"

"I don't care whether you know him or not." Trudy's tone was urgent. "We can't leave an old man to wait alone. I can't stay with him, and there's no one else."

"But, Trudy—" Suddenly the impact hit Gretchen. "Oh, no. Trudy, is she . . ." Gretchen swallowed hard. "Is Susan going to . . ."

"They're very hopeful," Trudy answered. "But heart surgeons don't give guarantees. Now hurry up."

Gretchen fought back tears all the way to the hospital. Her fears for Susan and her memories of her little sister's death mixed together until she finally had to sit in the hospital parking lot by herself for several minutes to get herself together. Before she took the elevator up to the surgical floor, she stopped in the bathroom and washed her face. "Nancy's death is in the past, and that's where it belongs," she told her reflection in the mirror. "For once you're going to forget your own problems and do something for somebody else."

When Gretchen walked into the surgical waiting room, John Halvorsen was sitting alone staring out the window. She hesitated before she approached him.

"Mr. Halvorsen?" She managed a smile as she sat down beside him. "I'm Gretchen Bauer. I'm a friend of Susan's—she also knows me as Clara the Clown."

John Halvorsen's eyes lighted in recognition and he took her hand. "I'm glad you're here," he said simply.

When she saw how alone the old man had been, Gretchen was glad, too. She knew he needed someone to share the waiting, no matter what the outcome. An image of a pair of roller skates shoved under a hospital bed flashed through her mind. To Gretchen, they'd become a symbol of hope. More than anything she wanted Susan to wear them again.

"Have you had any word?" she asked. She didn't know what she would do if the news was bad. John Halvorsen looked old and drawn and worried.

"A nurse comes in every few minutes and keeps me posted," he said. "Last time she told me Susan was doing fine and had maybe another hour to go."

The nurse had to be Trudy making sure he was all right, Gretchen decided. "That sounds very encouraging," she said.

"Too soon to tell," Mr. Halvorsen replied solemnly. "I just try to let the time go by and not think too much about what's happening in there."

"That sounds like a wise approach."

"Maybe you should do the same before you choke that chair to death," he suggested.

Gretchen followed his gaze to her knuckles, which were white from clutching the chair arms. She self-consciously clasped her hands in her lap. "I have a hard time not thinking about it," she admitted. "It's easier when I'm wearing the clown costume."

Mr. Halvorsen studied her quietly. "Maybe the clown face doesn't hide as much as you think. Susan told me Clara loves her."

Gretchen shifted uncomfortably. "She's a very perceptive little girl."

"Did you know she thinks Clara is her own private clown, and she's planning to take you home when she leaves the hospital?" Mr. Halvorsen asked.

Gretchen laughed. "No, she hasn't told me about that yet."

"She also says you know Dr. Carson. He's been real nice to her, too."

At the mention of Alex's name, Gretchen tensed. She hadn't thought about him in a couple of hours, not since Trudy called. For more than a week he'd been all she thought about.

"I'm kind of expecting him to show up pretty soon," Mr. Halvorsen continued.

"Alex is coming here?" She'd never considered that Alex might be at the hospital. But, of course, he cared about Susan, too. Maybe more than she'd realized.

"When I phoned, he said he'd be here as soon as he could get away," Mr. Halvorsen explained, "but he runs that clinic on Saturdays and he had a bunch of kids waiting."

"I didn't know his Saturday patients were kids," Gretchen said thoughtfully. She'd assumed he had busy executives coming in on Saturdays.

"Yeah, he's probably seen hundreds of kids who would never have gone to a dentist if they'd had to pay."

Gretchen sat forward, not sure she understood. "You mean the dental work is free?"

"I always pay him a little something when I can," Mr. Halvorsen answered quietly, "but I wouldn't have to."

Gretchen felt her cheeks flush with embarrassment. In all the time she'd lived with Alex, she'd assumed his primary goal was to make money. He'd never once mentioned the free clinic.

"Here's someone now." Mr. Halvorsen looked up expectantly as the waiting room door opened and Trudy appeared.

The expression on her face brought Gretchen to her feet. "What is it, Trudy? What did they say?"

"I just talked with the surgeon," Trudy began in a calm, professional voice, but Gretchen caught a glimpse of tears glistening in her eyes. "It's almost over and Susan's doing fine."

"Thank God," Gretchen breathed.

John Halvorsen was instantly on his feet. "Does that mean she's going to be all right?"

"Yes, Mr. Halvorsen," Trudy answered, "she's going to be all right."

"Hallelujah!" he shouted, the taut lines in his face drawing into a smile. He threw his arms around Gretchen and hugged her. "Hallelujah!" he whispered again.

Over the old man's shoulder, Gretchen saw Alex standing in the doorway, with a smile as big as her own.

12

"SHE'S ALL RIGHT?" Alex questioned, just to be sure.

"Oh, Alex, yes."

He folded Gretchen into his arms, and she felt relief surge through him as it had through her. Nothing else mattered right then except that the little girl who had struggled so hard had won her battle.

"I guess I got here a little late," Alex said, turning to Mr. Halvorsen.

"Nope, Dr. Carson, you're right on time. Gretchen here kept the watch with me, and you came along for the celebration."

Alex and Gretchen sat down on either side of Mr. Halvorsen and talked to him for nearly an hour before the surgeon came in, still in his scrub suit, to report that the operation had been a complete success. He said that after several weeks of convalescence Susan could go back to normal activities.

"That means she'll roller skate again," Gretchen said after the doctor left.

"I wasn't able to get Tweety in here to visit her," Alex added, "but now maybe we can take her out to Mother's to see him."

Gretchen met Alex's eyes. "Yes," she agreed tentatively. "Maybe we can."

John Halvorsen took both their hands and looked from one to the other. "Seems like you two know each other better than I realized," he observed with a quiet smile. "I'm going to wait till Susan wakes up, but why don't you go on now and get yourselves some lunch."

"We'll wait with you," Gretchen protested.

The old man shook his head firmly. "You come back and see Susan in a day or two. That'll make her happy."

Promising they'd come whenever they could, Alex and Gretchen took the elevator down to the hospital coffee shop. "I'm sorry I couldn't get here sooner," Alex said as he held the coffee shop door open for her. "This must have been very hard for you after what happened with your little sister."

Gretchen turned to him, startled. "You know, I haven't even thought about Nancy since I walked into that waiting room." For a moment, she felt guilty. Over the years she'd relived Nancy's death hundreds of times, whenever she walked into a hospital or encountered a sick child. Today should have been worse than all the others.

"Maybe you're getting rid of some of the ghosts," Alex observed.

Gretchen nodded thoughtfully. "Maybe I finally am."

As they walked through the cafeteria line, Alex picked up two sandwiches and a piece of chocolate layer cake while Gretchen selected a chef's salad.

"You do eat healthy food once in a while," Alex teased, as he looked at her lunch.

"My diet's perfectly adequate," Gretchen protested. She eyed his cake. "But maybe I'll go back for dessert."

The good-natured bickering that had marked their relationship from the beginning sent chills through Gretchen. She'd been totally caught up with her relief about Susan, but now that she was alone with Alex, all their problems came rushing back. First of all, she owed him an apology.

"I'm sorry I was such a bitch about you winning the lottery." She waited for his reaction. If she was hoping for instant forgiveness, she didn't get it.

"You were kind of a pain," he agreed.

"You wouldn't have liked it either, Yuppie, if you'd been in my shoes," she shot back.

"Nope."

"So why did you pay the rent? And the loan?"

He shrugged. "Without you I never would have bought the ticket. It was the least I could do."

Gretchen focused on eating her salad. So she'd been right from the beginning. He'd simply been fulfilling an obligation, just as she'd thought when she read his note. In the days since he'd moved out, she'd let herself hope his gesture might have meant something more.

"The timing on this thing worked out pretty well," Alex told her. "My condominium was ready when you threw me out. That was where I'd been planning to take you last Saturday."

Gretchen didn't look at him. "So you were going to leave anyway."

"Does that really matter?"

"No," Gretchen replied slowly, "I suppose it doesn't." But when she met his eyes, she got a different message. Not only was she lying, so was he. She reminded herself that nothing had changed. Even if his winning the lottery didn't make things worse, it didn't make them better, either. Logic told her she should leave well enough alone. Her heart told her otherwise. "I'd like to see your condominium some time," she added hesitantly. "Are you happy with it?"

"It's all right," Alex answered. "Would you really like to see it?"

She nodded, knowing she was heading into a brier patch but plunging on anyway.

"I'm going to be gone to a dental convention all week. Maybe you'd like to come next weekend," he suggested, "if you have any time free."

"I'll make time," she answered.

FOR THE NEXT SEVERAL DAYS, Gretchen felt as if she was floating on a cloud. No more loan shark, only an occasional late night and, best of all, Alex would be back soon, and she was going to see him. She was counting the days.

When the telephone rang early Wednesday afternoon, she answered with a cheery hello.

"Hello," said a strangely familiar female voice. "This is Lucille Carson."

As she clutched the telephone, Gretchen's palms turned to ice.

"I'm Alex Carson's mother."

Ever since she'd seen Alex at the hospital, all Gretchen had done was think about him. She had not thought about his background and she had completely repressed the memory of his mother. Gretchen swallowed. No words came out.

"Is this Gretchen?"

"Yes." Gretchen's voice squeaked. "This is Gretchen," she added, trying to sound somewhat more normal.

"I know we've barely met," the smooth, melodic voice on the other end continued, "but I feel almost as though I know you, dear. Alex has told me so much about you."

Fantastic! Gretchen thought. The only time she'd ever encountered his mother, she'd been wearing the French maid outfit. Alex had lied about her living there and hustled her out with a bag of sugar. She could just imagine the conversations they'd had about her since.

"The reason I'm calling, Gretchen," the voice continued, "is that I have an enormous favor to ask. I imagine Alex has told you all about his dental convention."

"He did mention it," Gretchen managed to respond.

"Well, then you know he won't be back until day after tomorrow, and that leaves me with a terrible dilemma. My sister, Amelia, has broken her hip and I'm flying out to Arizona this afternoon. But with Alex gone I have nowhere to leave Tweety."

Gretchen clamped her hand over the phone to mute the sounds of choking. Anything else, but not Tweety. She would have nothing to do with that stupid bird.

"I was wondering, dear," Mrs. Carson continued, "if you could fill in just until Alex gets back. I'd consider it such a favor—"

Gretchen cleared her throat. "Actually Mrs. Carson—"

"Oh please, call me Lucille."

"Actually, Lucille—" Gretchen didn't want to call her Lucille. "I really am gone quite a bit, especially at night, and I—"

"Don't give it another thought," Mrs. Carson interrupted. "Tweety keeps himself entertained. You should hear him sing. He has the most robust voice of any canary I've ever heard."

Gretchen thought *robust* was the most euphemistic description she'd ever heard. "You say Alex will be home day after tomorrow?" She hadn't expected him until Saturday. He must be coming home early.

"Yes, on Friday around noon. I do appreciate this so much. I'll just drop Tweety by on my way to the airport this afternoon, and maybe we can have a few minutes to get acquainted. Alex says you're living in his old apartment?"

So that was what he'd told his mother. Gretchen was tempted to blow the whole thing for him. "Yes, that's right," she answered sweetly.

"That will be perfect," Mrs. Carson said. "It's right on my way. I'll see you in just a little while."

Gretchen hung up the phone, wondering how she could be such a dummy. She wondered the same thing all over again as she scurried around the apartment with a dust cloth in one hand and the vacuum cleaner in the other. What difference did it make? It was just Alex's mother bringing a stupid, messy bird. Gretchen dusted faster, then hurried into the bedroom to change her clothes.

By the time the doorbell rang an hour later, Gretchen was wearing a pair of green linen slacks and a floral print blouse, the apartment was spotless, the coffee was ready and there was a batch of blueberry muffins in the oven. "I must have lost my mind," she muttered to herself as she hurried to answer the door.

Lucille Carson looked just as Gretchen remembered her. She was wearing a different dress, light blue instead of dusty pink, but the classic style was essentially the same. Again, the single word Gretchen could think of to describe it was *elegant*. "Do come in," she said. "Here, let me take the bird cage." Tweety fixed a beady eye on her, and Gretchen wondered if it was possible for a bird to know how she felt about it. She set the cage on the bookcase where it had been during Tweety's brief initial stay and offered Alex's mother a cup of coffee.

"It's so nice to have a chance to talk to you, Gretchen," Lucille said as she sat down. "Alex has told me so much about you."

"Exactly what has he told you?" Gretchen inquired. She knew it probably wasn't gracious to ask, but she wanted to know.

"Well, let's see. He said you're a teacher but you're temporarily between teaching jobs because of all the school cutbacks . . ."

That was a delicate way to put it, Gretchen thought.

"And he said in the meantime you're working as a performer to help put your sister through medical school." Mrs. Carson set down her cup and looked Gretchen in the eye. "I owe you an apology, Gretchen. The first time I met you, I was startled by your costume and I'm afraid I wasn't very nice."

"You were fine, there was no problem," Gretchen protested.

"No, Gretchen, I wasn't fine," Alex's mother said firmly. "I was acting like an overprotective mother making a snap judgment about the woman who was living with my son."

Gretchen's mouth dropped open. "You knew?"

"Oh, come. I don't know why your generation thinks my generation was born yesterday. My son does not keep dusting powder in the bathroom, a pink umbrella in the hall closet or sugared cereal in the kitchen. Nor does he have one bedroom door closed and say it's a storeroom. And that routine with the sugar—" Lucille Carson smiled. "Alex never was a convincing liar," she confided.

Gretchen giggled. "He still doesn't know you figured it out."

"Of course he doesn't. And I won't tell him if you won't."

"I don't know," Gretchen said as she picked up a blueberry muffin. "It might do him good." She was beginning to like Lucille Carson better. She obviously had more insight than Gretchen would have given her credit for.

"I hope you'll forgive the comparison, Gretchen, but you remind me very much of myself at your age."

"I what?" Maybe Alex's mother didn't have so much insight after all. "I'm afraid you're wrong there, Mrs. Carson, uh, Lucille. We're not anything alike."

"Why do you say that, Gretchen?"

"You have a magnificent home, you take trips abroad, you have everything. My background is...um...different."

Lucille Carson laughed, and Tweety, who had remained silent to that point, trilled two earsplitting octaves. Alex's mother stood up and firmly pulled on the cage cover. "You'll have an opportunity to enjoy Tweety later," she said. "Right now we need to clear up a misconception." When she turned toward Gretchen, her gaze was so direct that Gretchen looked away. "When I was your age, my dear, I was working as a waitress. I'd dropped out of college because I didn't have enough money to finish."

"You?" In her wildest dreams, Gretchen would never have envisioned Alex's mother as a waitress. She'd assumed Lucille Carson was the typical society matron whose family had always had money and position and always would. People like that didn't wait tables.

"Even after Alex's father and I were married, we struggled until his practice got going," Lucille Carson reminisced almost wistfully. "He didn't go in with an established dentist like Alex did."

"But you have so much," Gretchen said.

"Yes, my husband made some wise investments over the years, and since he's been gone they've continued to do well," Lucille said. "Don't misunderstand me, Gretchen. I enjoy being comfortable. But this is just a stage of life, and not necessarily the best one." She glanced around the small apartment, then at Gretchen. "The best time is where you are right now," she said, "when you're young and dreaming. No reality can ever match the dreams."

Gretchen didn't know what to say. She'd resented Lucille Carson from the moment they'd met because the woman was the epitome of everything she'd never had and assumed she never would. Now Mrs. Carson was telling her she was the one who was well off.

"Oh, dear, I have to run," Alex's mother said as she checked her watch. "The planes are usually late, but you never can count on it. It was so nice to have a chance to talk to you—I do hope you and Alex will come for dinner as soon as I get back."

"I'd like that," Gretchen answered, and realized that she really would. "And I'll take good care of Tweety," she promised as Lucille hurried down the stairs.

Gretchen's heart soared as she walked into the apartment. She'd never thought she could be so happy to have someone prove her wrong. Lucille Carson wasn't a cold society snob, which was exactly how Gretchen would have described her. Looks certainly could be deceiving.

Lucille as a waitress. Gretchen still couldn't quite get over that. She tried to imagine the woman thirty years younger, dressed in a white uniform with an apron tied around her waist and her hair, probably the same sandy brown as Alex's, pulled back into a net, her arms laden with plates of steaming food as she hurried across a crowded restaurant. Gretchen was able to conjure up the picture, but it bore no more relation to the gracious woman who'd just left her apartment than Gretchen herself in her red silk dress had to Clara the Clown.

Gretchen suddenly realized that during the entire discussion Lucille hadn't once mentioned Alex winning the lottery. Gretchen shook her head. Apparently, he hadn't even told her.

Removing the cover from Tweety's cage, Gretchen laughed as she studied the canary from a new perspective. He was still the weirdest-looking bird she'd ever seen, and she was never going to like him, but she didn't hate him any more, either. Tweety trilled a scale. He must like laughter, Gretchen decided. She had a feeling he was going to hear more of it.

GRETCHEN WAS ALREADY UP the next morning when Trudy pounded on the door.

"I knew you were awake because I heard the bird all the way down the hall—" Trudy began apologetically.

"This is two early morning visits in a week," Gretchen said cheerfully. "And I see you brought your own coffee this time," she noted as Trudy walked in with her coffee mug in one hand and the newspaper in the other.

"Just wait till you see what's in the paper this time!" Trudy had a gleam in her eye as she thrust the newspaper at Gretchen, who sat down on the couch and checked the headlines. "Congress Weighs Tax Bill...Bank Robber Gets One Million...Drug Giving New Hope To Bald Men...."

"Not there," Trudy said impatiently. "Turn to page six. You're not going to believe it."

Gretchen paged obediently through the newspaper. When she got to page six, she didn't have to ask what she was looking for. "That's Alex!" she shouted. "He must have picked up his money. But the headline says 'Millionaire for a Day.'"

"Keep reading." Trudy leaned over the back of the couch and pointed to the small story under the picture.

"'Alex Carson, 30, an Arlington, Virginia, dentist, became an instant millionaire today when he cashed in his winning lottery ticket. The money will be paid out in tax-free increments of $119,247.32 over the next twenty years,'" Gretchen read aloud.

"The next paragraph is the part that's going to blow your mind," Trudy predicted.

"'But Carson says his millionaire status will be brief,'" Gretchen continued. "'He already has arranged for the bulk of the money to be transferred into a trust fund to provide grants for needy medical students specializing in pediatric cardiology.'"

"Pediatric cardiology?" Gretchen repeated. She dropped the paper and stared at Trudy. "My God!" she whispered.

"See, I told you it was going to blow your mind." Trudy waved her arms, nearly spilling her coffee. "That yuppie dentist, as you call him, is giving away most of his winnings to help people like your sister."

"My God!" Gretchen exclaimed again. She picked up the paper and skimmed the rest of the article in which Alex defended his choice of charities to an obviously skeptical reporter by saying, "We owe our children the best medical care we can give them, and there's no better way to provide it than to invest in their future doctors."

She looked again at the picture of Alex, grinning broadly as he held a check out in front of him. Suddenly she knew he was grinning at her.

"Now tell me the hunk isn't a great guy," Trudy said jubilantly. "Just tell me."

"I can't believe he did that." Gretchen was still overwhelmed. "I thought I knew him . . ." Gretchen stopped. She'd thought a lot of things. She'd thought Alex was only interested in money. She'd thought he spent his Saturday charging fancy fees to business executives. She'd thought his mother was a super snob. She'd thought . . . She shook her head. "Damn, I've been so stupid, Trudy."

"I don't know that I'd call you stupid, exactly," Trudy said as she finished her coffee, "but you sure weren't any whiz kid. What are you going to do now?"

Gretchen didn't hesitate. "Alex is coming home tomorrow. When he gets there, Tweety and I are going to be waiting on his doorstep."

GRETCHEN WAS HALFWAY to Alex's condominium when she realized she'd forgotten Tweety's cage cover. From the back seat of her Volkswagen, Tweety sang all the way there, serenading the motorists at every stoplight, the clerk in the drugstore where Gretchen stopped to buy the mirror and the carpet tape, then the receptionist in Alex's building. A man riding up the elevator with them clapped his hands over his ears to shut out the bird's earsplitting song. What got to Gretchen was that she didn't care. Every time Tweety sang, she laughed, and he sang louder.

She wished she had a key to Alex's condominium, but since she didn't, she'd have to do the best she could. She set Tweety's cage down outside Alex's door and rang the bell, just to make sure he wasn't home yet. When he didn't answer, she removed the mirror and the roll of carpet tape from the drugstore bag. She ripped off a strip of tape and stuck the mirror in the center of Alex's door. Then she took a pencil and a pad of sticky notes out of her purse.

Dear Alex,
I want you to know how much I appreciate

Gretchen wadded up the paper and stuck it in her pocket. That wasn't right at all. She tried again.

Dear Alex,
There is so much I've learned in the past few days

She wadded up that one, too, and stuffed it into her pocket. After three more unsuccessful attempts, she threw down the pencil and paced up and down the hall. None of that was what she wanted to say to Alex. But what did she want to say? Tweety chirped and pecked at his birdseed dish, scattering seed on the hall carpet. Finally, after nearly ten minutes, Gretchen picked up the pencil and scribbled furiously. Right or wrong, it was how she felt.

A.
I love you, Yuppie, in spite of everything.

G.

She smoothed the note in the center of the mirror, picked up Twooty and disappeared behind the door to the emergency stairway. Alex might as well know exactly how she felt, and then, if he didn't share those feelings, well... She'd cry later.

Gretchen waited nearly an hour before the elevator doors opened and she heard footsteps in the hall. She listened carefully. The footsteps stopped just about where Alex's door should be. For several moments there was silence. Gretchen's heart pounded louder and louder. She expected a key to turn in a lock, more footsteps, something.

Then came a shout she could have heard three floors below. "Gretchen!" Alex bellowed. "Where are you?"

She couldn't get there fast enough. The moment Alex saw her, he swept her into his arms and whirled her around with such vigor that his reaction to winning the lottery paled by comparison. "I love you," he whispered, and then he shouted, "I love you." He kissed her on the mouth until she was breathless, then held her away from him and looked at her. "Damn, I've missed you, Gretchen."

"Oh, Alex, me, too. The apartment was so quiet and so empty and I didn't trip over your bike and I hated every minute of it."

"And I missed the smell of your dusting powder and the underwear in the bathtub," he told her as he unlocked the door and pushed it open in one swift motion. "But mostly I missed you." Before she could protest, he lifted her off the floor as though she weighed nothing at all, carried her inside and kicked the door shut behind them.

"Alex, what are you doing?"

"I'm making up for lost time," he told her, striding quickly across the carpet.

"Put me down!" she demanded, burying her face in his neck and not struggling at all.

"Anything you say," he agreed and dropped her directly in the center of his new, king-size bed.

"But, Alex—"

Gretchen didn't have a chance to say anything more. His mouth was on hers, hot and familiar and feeding the hunger inside her. She held on to him as if she might never let him go. "I didn't mean those things I said," she murmured.

"None of that matters now," he told her. He was beside her on the bed, his lips caressing her neck. "All I want is you."

"Oh, Alex, me, too." She rolled against him, molding her body into his to feel his desire. She wiggled sideways. She wanted more.

"You like that," he said.

"You know I like that."

He raised up enough to unbutton her blouse, slipping his hand inside as he moved downward, one button at a time.

She pressed harder against him, her hips moving. "Oh, God, Alex." She shuddered as the blouse fell away and his fingers pushed aside her wispy lace bra. "You know all the right places."

"Damn right," he answered, his mouth and his hands busy. He touched her everywhere, unbuttoning, undressing, while she did the same.

"You're wearing some of my favorite underwear," Gretchen noted as she tugged at the band of his shorts. "But I like it better off."

"Then go ahead," he urged, lying back and raising his hips.

She didn't hesitate. "It's really tight," she said, following the front seam with her fingers.

He groaned. "And getting tighter every minute. Take it off, Gretchen."

She took it off, slowly, tantalizingly, following the fabric with her fingers until he couldn't stand it any longer. He gripped her hips with his hands and raised her above him, then carefully brought her body down.

Bracing her hands on his shoulders, she watched dark passion in his eyes as her body began to move, slowly at first and then faster, matching his responses and her own. At the final moment, his hands tightened around her hips and his body arched high into hers before she collapsed on top of him.

"OH, ALEX, I COULD DO THAT all day and tonight and tomorrow and forever," she told him afterward as she lay nestled in his arms.

"Maybe we will." He ran his fingers in whisper-soft strokes across her breasts. "I can't get enough of you. I tried to put you out of my mind, Gretchen, but you wouldn't go. I must have picked up the phone a hundred times."

"But why didn't you call, Alex?"

"Because you threw me out." He leaned back on one elbow and looked at her curiously. "What happened? What changed your mind?"

Gretchen smiled at him. "I finally figured out what an idiot I was."

"I won't argue that." He toyed idly with her breast until Gretchen drew in a sharp breath. "But there must have been something that sparked the revelation," he continued. "Was it the trust fund I set up?"

"That trust fund was a wonderful thing for you to do, Alex," Gretchen told him, "but it was just one of a whole lot of things." When she ran over them in her mind, Gretchen realized it was no wonder her whole outlook had changed. The first jolt had come when Susan's grandfather told her about Alex's free clinic. She'd also come to terms with her own past the day of Susan's surgery. On top of all that, she'd found out how empty life was with Alex gone. And then there had been the visit from Lucille Carson. Gretchen traced lazy figure eights across Alex's chest. "If I had to pick one thing, other than missing you," she said slowly, "it would be your mother."

"My mother?"

"Yep. She came to bring—" With a gasp, Gretchen sat up. "Alex, my God! I forgot about Tweety."

"What about Tweety?"

"He's outside, at least he'd better be outside. Quick, give me my clothes." She spotted Alex's robe on a chair by the bed and grabbed it. She wrapped it around her as she raced through the apartment, leaving Alex behind her pulling on his pants. But the minute she opened the door, she knew everything was all right. Although his song was muffled by the heavy fire door, Tweety was definitely there.

Alex was standing in the doorway of his condominium, bare-chested and without his shoes, when she returned moments later carrying the bird cage with Tweety in it singing lustily. "Maybe you should bring your suitcase inside, too," she suggested calmly. "We seem to have been in a bit of a hurry the first time we went in."

"Gretchen," Alex demanded as he picked up the suitcase, "where the hell did you get that damned bird?"

"From your mother," Gretchen replied sweetly. "She's off to Arizona because Aunt Amelia broke her hip, and she asked me to bring Tweety to you."

"No!" Alex exclaimed firmly, as he closed the door. "I will not baby-sit the bird. I made that clear the last time."

"Now, Alex," Gretchen soothed, raising her voice to make herself heard over Tweety's singing. "He's not so bad. You can put a throw rug down to catch the birdseed, and every time you laugh he'll sing to you. And sometimes when you don't laugh, he'll sing anyway."

"I know all about Tweety," Alex growled, as he watched Gretchen set the bird cage on a small table in the entry hall. "He's messy, loud and obnoxious."

"I believe your mother's word for it is 'robust,'" Gretchen teased.

"Wait a minute." Alex took hold of her arm and turned her toward him. "Why are you defending the bird? What else did you and my mother talk about?"

"We had a lovely conversation over muffins and coffee and some day I'll tell you all about it. Now I want to see your condominium." She took a step toward the living room and glanced around. "It looks just like when you moved into my apartment," she said impishly. "A vast wasteland of packing cartons and sports equipment."

"Smart-ass," he retorted, taking her in his arms. He studied her face, which had become so very special to him, and hoped he'd picked the right time and place for what he was about to say. "Gretchen," he asked softly, "will you marry me?"

"Marry you?" Her blue eyes were wide. "Right now?"

"Yes, right now. And then move into the condominium with me so we can trip over your boxes, too, and you'll quit bugging me about mine."

He shot her that rakish grin of his and Gretchen burst out laughing. "I guess I could do worse, Yuppie." Tweety trilled an enthusiastic scale as Alex took her in his arms.

HARLEQUIN *Temptation*

COMING NEXT MONTH

#265 SECOND TO NONE Rita Clay Estrada

Brad Bartholomew's father and Gina O'Con's
mother had shared a deep and forbidden love for
twenty years. As if destined to recreate their
passion, Brad and Gina were inexorably drawn to
each other, even though the past might stand
between them....

#266 MACNAMARA AND HALL Elise Title

When next-door-neighbors Tracy Hall and Tom
Macnamara got together to coach their kids' little
league team, they quickly discovered they were a
hit *off* the diamond, too. In fact, it was clear from
the outset that Tom and Tracy's love was heading
for the big leagues!

#267 BEST-LAID PLANS Mary Tate Engels

Mayor Lacy Donahue had a winning strategy for
revitalizing Silverton, New Mexico: Holt
Henderson. Holt's talent at restoration could
change the face of the small mining town. But
Holt's devastating appeal could topple Lucy's
reserve. And that was something her honor hadn't
planned on.

#268 CODE NAME: CASANOVA
Dawn Carroll

Agent Daniel Avanti was the most charming devil
who had ever walked the earth. Kerith Anders
was his last assignment before he retired the code
name Casanova.

You'll flip . . . your pages won't!
Read paperbacks *hands-free* with

Book Mate·I

The perfect "mate" for all your romance paperbacks

Traveling • Vacationing • At Work • In Bed • Studying • Cooking • Eating

Perfect size for all standard paperbacks, this wonderful invention makes reading a pure pleasure! Ingenious design holds paperback books OPEN and FLAT so even wind can't ruffle pages— leaves your hands free to do other things. Reinforced, wipe-clean vinyl-covered holder flexes to let you turn pages without undoing the strap . . . supports paperbacks so well, they have the strength of hardcovers!

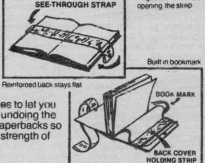

Pages turn WITHOUT opening the strap

SEE-THROUGH STRAP

Reinforced back stays flat

Built in bookmark

BOOK MARK

BACK COVER HOLDING STRIP

10 x 7¼ opened
Snaps closed for easy carrying, too

Available now. Send your name, address, and zip code, along with a check or money order for just $5.95 + 75¢ for postage & handling (for a total of $6.70) payable to Reader Service to:

Reader Service
Bookmate Offer
901 Fuhrmann Blvd.
P.O. Box 1396
Buffalo, N.Y. 14269-1396

Offer not available in Canada
*New York and Iowa residents add appropriate sales tax

BM-G

SWEEPSTAKES RULES & REGULATIONS

NO PURCHASE NECESSARY TO ENTER OR RECEIVE A PRIZE

1 To enter and join the Reader Service, check off the "YES" box on your Sweepstakes Entry Form and return to Harlequin Reader Service. If you do not wish to join the Reader Service but wish to enter the Sweepstakes only, check off the "NO" box on your Sweepstakes Entry Form. Incomplete and/or inaccurate entries are ineligible for that section or sections(s) of prizes. Not responsible for mutilated or unreadable entries or inadvertent printing errors. Mechanically reproduced entries are null and void. Be sure to also qualify for the Bonus Sweepstakes. See rule #3 on how to enter

2. Either way, your unique Sweepstakes number will be compared against the list of winning numbers generated at random by the computer. In the event that all prizes are not claimed, random drawings will be held from all entries received from all presentations to award all unclaimed prizes. All cash prizes are payable in U.S. funds. This is in addition to any free, surprise or mystery gifts that might be offered. The following prizes are offered: *Grand Prize (1) $1,000,000 Annuity; First Prize (1) $35,000; Second Prize (1) $10,000; Third Prize (3) $5,000; Fourth Prize (10) $1,000; Fifth Prize (25) $500; Sixth Prize (5,000) $5.

   * This Sweepstakes contains a Grand Prize offering of a $1,000,000 annuity. Winner may elect to receive $25,000 a year for 40 years without interest; totalling $1,000,000 or $350,000 in one cash payment. Entrants may cancel Reader Service at any time without cost or obligation to buy.

3. Extra Bonus Prize: This presentation offers two extra bonus prizes valued at $30,000 each to be awarded in a random drawing from all entries received. To qualify, scratch off the silver on your Lucky Keys. If the registration numbers match, you are eligible for the prize offering.

4. Versions of this Sweepstakes with different graphics will be offered in other mailings or at retail outlets by Torstar Corp. and its affiliates. This promotion is being conducted under the supervision of Marden-Kane, Inc., an independent judging organization. By entering this Sweepstakes, each entrant accepts and agrees to be bound by these rules and the decisions of the judges, which shall be final and binding. Odds of winning in the random drawing are dependent upon the total number of entries received. Taxes, if any, are the sole responsibility of the winners. Prizes are nontransferable. All entries must be received by March 31, 1990. The drawing will take place on or about April 30, 1990 at the offices of Marden-Kane, Inc., Lake Success, N.Y.

5. This offer is open to residents of the U.S., United Kingdom and Canada, 18 years or older, except employees of Torstar Corp., its affiliates, subsidiaries, Marden-Kane and all other agencies and persons connected with conducting this Sweepstakes. All Federal, State and local laws apply. Void wherever prohibited or restricted by law.

6. Winners will be notified by mail and may be required to execute an affidavit of eligibility and release, which must be returned within 14 days after notification. Canadian winners will be required to answer a skill-testing question. Winners consent to the use of their name, photograph and/or likeness for advertising and publicity in conjunction with this or similar promotions, without additional compensation.

7 For a list of our most current major prize winners, send a stamped, self-addressed envelope to: Winners List, c/o Marden-Kane, Inc., P.O. Box 701, Sayreville, N.J. 08871

If Sweepstakes entry form is missing, please print your name and address on a 3″ × 5″ piece of plain paper and send to:

In the U.S.	In Canada
Sweepstakes Entry	Sweepstakes Entry
901 Fuhrmann Blvd.	P.O. Box 609
P.O. Box 1867	Fort Erie, Ontario
Buffalo, NY 14269-1867	L2A 5X3

LTY-H89
© 1988 Harlequin Enterprises Ltd